ALONG CAME THE GIRL

GRACIE YORK

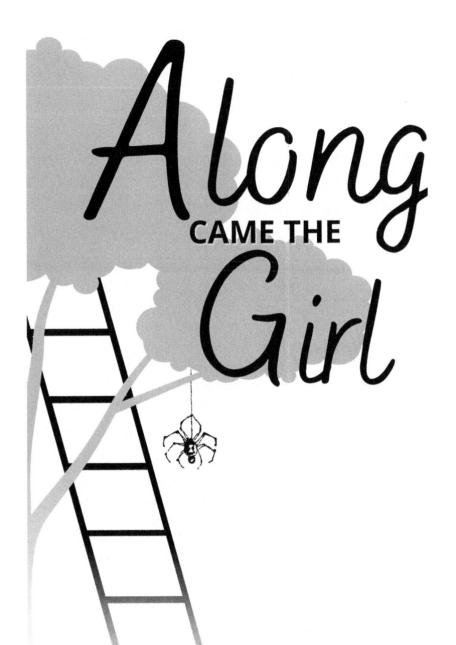

Along

CAME THE

Girl

JENNI BARA AND AJ RANNEY WRITING AS
GRACIE YORK

Along Came the Girl

Copyright @ 2023 Gracie York

All rights reserved.

Line, Copy, Proofreading by Beth Lawton at VB Edits

Interior formatting by H.C. PA & Formatting Services

ISBN: 979-8-9859485-8-5 (ebook)

ISBN: 978-1-959389-10-1 (paperback)

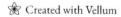 Created with Vellum

*To everyone who has had a rough year,
remember the best things happen
when plans go to shit.*

1

Pregnancy Week One:

You're listening to your boss lecture about no drama with no clue the hurricane of drama you're about to bring.

Owen

"RULE NUMBER TWO: no drama and no bullshit. You hear me, McKinley?" The chair creaked as my new chief rocked back and crossed his arms with a glare.

I fisted my hands in my lap. Although my position with the quintessential small-town firehouse wasn't my idea of a dream job, rule number two sounded perfect. After the way my last six months had gone, I'd have to be a moron to get involved with any type of drama. I'd transferred to escape the mess that my life had become in Richmond. Now I wanted peace. *Not* chaos.

After a quick raise of his chin, Brian Thompson went on.

"You moved up quickly through the ranks at Richmond 15. I can appreciate how dedicated you were."

"Thanks, Chief." But I didn't miss the *were*. Sitting up a bit straighter, I continued. "I'll show this house the same commitment."

But instead of smiling, Brian pursed his lips. "I've heard the rumors. Career focused, single-mindedly driven. I expect you have your sights set on my job."

I couldn't deny it. In Richmond, I had been a Lieutenant. My goal had been to be the first fire chief under forty in the city. I clenched my jaw, once again regretting the choices that had led me to Half Moon Lake. The small town wasn't utter shit or anything. I'd vacationed here a few times with friends, and it was gorgeous in the summer. But starting over wasn't ideal.

7

And here I was, prepared to bust my ass in Bumfuck, North Carolina to earn stripes that should have already belonged to me.

The chief leaned forward, resting his thick forearms on the desk. "Part of why I brought you on was so we could work together, and depending on how that goes, maybe I can groom you for my job someday. I won't hold the bullshit you left behind against you. I get not everything that happened was your fault."

Of course it wasn't my fault. Daddy's princess snapped her fingers, and I was the one who paid the price.

"Lesson learned there, sir." I assured my new boss. "Just want to come in and do my job."

The chief nodded. "You're not a rookie, but you are the new guy. You'll earn a place here in time. But until then, the guys will give you shit and the jobs they usually hand out to candidates. My two cents? Show them you want to be here and that you're ready to earn your spot. That'll go over better than reminding them that you technically outrank them."

I dipped my chin and held back the *you've got to be kidding me* that I wanted so badly to let fly. I needed this to work, and I hated to admit that the chief was probably right.

"Your EMT training will be an asset here. The guys will see that pretty quickly."

The EMT certification had given me opportunities to pick up extra shifts in Richmond. Plus, all the top-level guys had it. I'd been successful in fast-tracking my career in every way but one. In my lap, my knuckles were white, so I forced myself to relax.

Chief Thompson balanced his chin on his fist as he studied me, and I tried not to fidget under the intensity. Although the man was probably close to sixty, he was still solid and tall and broad-shouldered. Even with his blond hair going silver, the man was intimidating. He dropped his hand to the desk and sighed.

"How's the new apartment working out?" His hazel eyes softened, and his lips turned up at the corners. Almost as if he'd taken off his boss hat and had put on one more fitting for a friend.

That would take a hot minute for me to get used to. My previous chief had run a house three times the size of this one, and in a major city. Heart-to-hearts and friendships with superiors didn't happen at the station in the city.

"It's great. I'm glad you suggested the place." The chief had given me the name of an apartment complex not far from the station. On a nice day, I could even walk if I wanted.

"I've heard good things." He nodded. "You all unpacked?"

I'd unpacked the day the moving truck arrived. I couldn't stand living out of boxes. And I'd never understood how it took people weeks to organize their shit. The chaos of it all would have driven me insane.

"I got that done the second I got here." I chuckled.

"A man after my own heart. My daughter used to make me insane with all her clutter." Although he was criticizing his daughter, the man's smile implied that she was the apple of his eye. "Well," the chief huffed, pulling himself out of his chair, "let's go meet the crew."

We stood almost eye to eye. More often than not, I was the tallest man in the room at six-foot three, but the chief stood taller. It was weird to look up at someone. Almost intimidating. I swallowed those thoughts down and walked in to meet the guys.

A clap of the chief's hands had all four men sitting at a small circular table turning. They were all dressed in heather T-shirts and navy pants, playing what looked like rummy.

"McKinley." Chief Thompson tipped his head toward me,

then he pointed to each of the guys. "Ricktor, Stoer, Mitchell, Murray."

The man farthest from us pushed his chair back and stood, wearing a smirk that could have been welcoming or trouble, I wasn't sure. But his brown eyes seemed friendly as he moved closer.

"Jason. You can call me Jay. I hear you're taking over shift lead for us." It was a challenge, but he held out his hand. "You better not suck."

I shook his hand. "I only suck when she's begging for it." I forced my signature eat shit smile and got a couple of laughs. "I'm Owen."

Jay chuckled. "I don't care what your name is. I'm going to call you new guy."

"Mitchell," the chief growled. "What's my rule?"

The young guy finger gunned him and winked. "Don't fuck with your daughter. She's off limits."

The chief shook his head. "Not that one." He turned to me. "Good luck with these assholes."

All the guys smiled and stood. And I was ready. For a new job and a new town.

Miles and miles away from Richmond and drama and bad decisions.

2

Pregnancy Week Two and Half:

 Go ahead and drink all those shots now because you won't get to again for at least nine months.

CeCe

"ARE you sure you should have another margarita?" I asked my best friend.

Kelly frowned at her empty drink like it held all the world's secrets. Finally, she shrugged, sending her long brown hair bouncing. "Celebrating means *te-qui-la.*" She did a little shake that was probably supposed to be dancing. But drunk Kelly was a hot mess.

I chuckled. Because *sober* Kelly was a hot mess. Drunk Kelly was Jack's problem.

"You literally said Jack was going to be the *responsible* one." Kelly rolled her eyes and leaned into her boyfriend, who just smirked and took a sip of the beer he was nursing.

I shook my head. Kelly was the throw caution to the wind friend. The *let's just do it*, live life to the fullest, ridiculous friend everyone should have. My idea of fun was diagnosing a tricky case or helping to set a broken arm. Or, if I was really lucky, shadowing the head of the ER for the day.

That was why I loved our friendship. I needed someone to push me to relax and let loose more often. But we were already two margaritas in the hole.

"Last time I was big fun instead of the voice of reason, we missed our flight home from Florida."

"Oh my gosh, are we still in Florida?" Kelly scanned the room, her head whipping back and forth dramatically. "No, we're not," she deadpanned. "It all totes worked out. We didn't get locked in Florida forever because Cece was fun."

Her attitude wasn't shocking. Life happened to Kelly, and she rolled with it.

"There is no plane here for us to miss." Kelly waved me off. "So it's drinks and dancing, because we're celebrating us."

After my first week at the hospital in my new role as a physician assistant, I was looking forward to blowing off steam. But I couldn't shake the urge to seek out another plan. Something else to work toward. My list had been with me since I was a freshman in high school.

Be the valedictorian of my high school class, check.

Go to UNC Chapel Hill, check.

Graduate with honors and get into the master's program, check, check.

Become a physician assistant and work in the ER, check and check.

I liked goals. They fit me. But I'd achieved everything I'd been working for over the last several years. And now I didn't know what to do. I had no next move. It was unsettling.

"Why do you look thought constipated? It's drinks, not the cure for everything messed up in the world." Kelly threw her hands in the air. "I wouldn't survive if I had to overthink as much as you do."

Jack, all too aware of Kelly's lack of logical thought, coughed on a laugh.

Kelly sent him a side-eye, but he just threw his arm over her shoulder and kissed her temple.

"I'm not overthinking. But I just—like, what am I supposed to do now?"

"Drink." Kelly's expression said *duh*. "Dance." She frowned. "Remember, *be* the big fun." She pushed away from the table. "This is an emergency for real. We, like, sups *need* shots."

"Shots?"

"Yes." Kelly rolled her eyes and shook her head. "No great night ever started with 'hey, let's get a round of waters.'" Before Jack or I could respond, she headed toward the bar.

"Should you be concerned about that?" I nodded to my friend.

"I'm sober. I'll make sure you're both okay. We have a driver to get us home anyway. and"—Jack's bright green eyes shone as he smirked—"tequila makes her clothes fall off. That's a win every time."

Ugh. Jack and Kelly were grossly cute. I hated to be jealous of my best friend. It wasn't that I wanted Jack. But the idea of having someone *like* Jack tugged at me. Before I could sink further into my depressing thoughts, my friend was back with a round of shots and *another* margarita.

After a toast that didn't make sense, Kelly dragged me out onto the dance floor.

Tomorrow's worries were starting to feel far away. Maybe Kelly was right about overthinking. I should enjoy today, especially after I'd worked so hard in grad school and to get my certifications and land my dream job. I deserved to let loose and blow off some steam now and then.

Six songs later, we were back at the high-top with fresh drinks.

"We're totes doing the cruise this winter." Kelly, unwilling to just sit, jumped onto her toes and wobbled a bit.

"I should have time once the calcium water goes live in November." Jack steadied Kelly and pushed her drink back so she wouldn't hit it with her waving hands.

We'd talked about going on a cruise in May, but Kelly had started a new job at Hill Water in March and couldn't take the time off. Then Jack got busy with the launch of Hill Water's new project, and he couldn't get off.

"We'll find a time." I picked up the margarita glass, but

before I could raise it to my mouth, movement on the table caught my attention, and I jerked with a shriek. A spider was coming right for me.

I shoved my stool back, smacking into the solid wall of someone's back. My margarita flew out of my hand as I scrambled to get farther away from the table, and the stool toppled to the floor. My foot caught in the leg, and I teetered.

"Icy," came a deep voice, as strong hands settled at my waist and caught me before I hit the ground.

I spun, burying my face in the chest of the huge man. I clawed at his shirt and yanked him closer.

He coughed. Or maybe he gasped; I didn't know. I didn't care. I needed to get away from the monster.

"Whoa." The man planted his feet and held firm. "What are you doing?"

"Ew. Ew. Ew. We have to go." I fisted my hands in his shirt, clutching for dear life as I peeked back at the table. Someone *had* to get rid of it.

"*Why?*" His arm settled around my waist. "Is someone trying to hurt you?"

"Yes," I hissed. "With its millions of eyes and too many appendages, it has all the advantages."

Jack cleared his throat, and I peered behind me, still holding tight to the broad chest.

Jack held up a napkin with the eight-legged demon squished inside. And if I wasn't mistaken, he was fighting a grin.

I let out a breath and relaxed my shoulders. It was dead. I didn't need to panic. I tipped my head back, finally realizing I was clinging to a stranger, and my heart once again stopped.

Dark blue orbs were intent on me. The air around me and this man sparked with electricity.

Wow. This guy was gorgeous. His clean-shaven, chiseled jaw, blue eyes, and dark hair made such a striking combination. And I was currently tucked in his arms.

"You terrified of spiders, Little Miss Muffet?" The guy smirked.

My cheeks burned. Now that the thing was dead, I could admit to my overreaction.

"Ridiculously," I mumbled, releasing the poor guy's shirt and trying to smooth out the wrinkles in the gray material.

But he didn't release my waist. Instead, he used his free hand to force my chin up. The move sent that current of electricity shooting through me once again.

Damn. This man exuded sexual energy.

"It's cute." His eyes danced. "I'm Owen."

"Cece." I flattened my hand on his chest so I could step back, wincing as I came into contact with cold, wet fabric. Not only had I acted like a lunatic, but I'd also doused him. "Oh, shoot. You're wearing my drink."

"Stellar aim. You gave me a nice cold shower before I had any idea what the hell was going on," he teased.

She grimaced. "Sorry."

"Don't be. Have a drink with me, and we'll call it even." His smile sent a host of chills up my spine. There was no way I could resist.

I nodded. "Let me get them. It's the least I can do."

He tilted his head to the side and licked his lips. "Seems safer if I'm the one holding the cold liquid." His teasing smirk flipped my stomach. "Be right back." He knocked his knuckles on the table.

I hardly had time to take in his long fingers before he turned. But my gaze stayed locked on his back as he walked toward the bar. The gray T-shirt he wore pulled tight across his wide shoulders and dropped to a narrow waist, and hands-down, he had the best ass I'd ever seen in a pair of jeans. I wanted to sink my teeth into it.

Where did that come from? I'd love to claim it was alcohol, but although I was tipsy, I wasn't drunk.

A chuckle came from across the high-top, and I turned back to Kelly and Jack.

"Now, *that* is so what you need."

Heat crept back into my face, and I dropped my attention to the floor and righted the stool to avoid my friends' assessing gazes. I hated my pale skin. It always gave me away. Luckily, Kelly didn't push as I slid the stool back to the table and sat.

"Come on, Jack. Let's head home." Kelly wrapped her fingers around her boyfriend's bicep, but he didn't move, just crossed his arms on the tabletop. "Do you really want to mess this up for her?"

"Maybe." He frowned. "We don't know this guy." His focus was locked on the bar behind me.

Kelly scoffed. "I didn't know you when I agreed to be your fake fiancée, and look how well that worked out."

"Yes, but—" Jack slammed his mouth shut and ground his teeth.

I chuckled.

"What?" Kelly asked.

Jack shook his head. But I knew what he'd almost let slip. There was no way Jack would let someone he cared about agree to go away for a weekend and pretend to be engaged to a stranger. Jack stressed about things, while Kelly wondered why people worried.

"Why don't you close out the tab?" he suggested in a clear ploy to distract Kelly from the topic.

She cocked her head to the side. "What?"

"The credit card is still at the bar."

With a wave of her hand, she dismissed Jack. "They usually keep it for a day or two and then call me to get it."

That was how Kelly handled tabs. And I was shocked that Jack didn't know that yet.

"No." He shook his head. "That is *not* what we're doing."

Kelly sighed. "Oh my God, everyone's going to wonder why

I don't trust them anymore if I start taking my cards home with me."

I disguised a laugh as a cough as Jack's eye twitched.

"Tell them your boyfriend is weird. But please get our credit card, crazy girl."

She sighed and rolled her eyes, then skipped off to the bar without another word.

Jack blew out a long breath. My best friend drove him nuts, but he loved every minute of it.

I chuckled. "You two are hashtag life goals."

He dropped his elbows to the wooden high-top. "Can I talk you into leaving with us? I can have Stan drop you off at your place."

I scrunched my nose. Talk about being a third wheel. I didn't mind hanging out with them. And Jack's driver, who'd moved here from LA when Jack did, was nice, but when given the choice of a drink with a hot guy or a car ride as the third wheel, there was no contest.

"I've been to plenty of bars alone. I'm okay." I glanced over my shoulder at Owen, who was making his way back to me, wearing the sexiest smirk and carrying two fresh margaritas. "Really, I'm good."

Owen set the drinks down and traded introductions with Jack, then turned back to me.

"Your friend told me to be the kind of big fun that makes you miss your flight?"

He leaned his forearm on the table, drawing my attention to the corded muscles. They rippled as he lifted his drink. Watching his full lips slip around the rim of the glass as he took a sip sent a new round of shivers up my spine. And my breath caught when his tongue swiped along his lower lip.

"Are you catching a plane?"

"Nope." I lifted my margarita. "And we'd need six more of these before Kelly makes sense to you."

He chuckled.

"One more round before we bounce." Kelly dropped four shots on the table and sent Jack a look. "And I got our card back, worrywart." She passed a glass to each of us and lifted her own high. "To running out of gas, missing the green light, and spilling your drink."

Owen froze for a beat before clinking his glass against mine. He was probably wondering about the kind of people who would drink to that nonsense.

But before I could translate the Kelly-speak, Jack did.

"Because the best things happen when plans go to shit."

We all tossed back their shots.

"Yup." I popped the *P* and fought back a giggle. Maybe that shot was a bad idea. When was the last time I'd drank this much?

Pondering that question, I scanned Owen's face, tracking over his smooth jaw, then down the column of his neck. If I was going to let loose tonight, I couldn't have imagined a hotter guy to do it with.

Kelly cleared her throat and tilted my head. "Have fun." It was more like a command than a statement. But she turned her eyes to Owen. "Remember what I said." Then she smirked at Jack. "Check your pocket, sexy." She kissed his cheek and sauntered away.

Jack slid a hand into his pocket, and his head swiveled between Kelly and me. "I'm sending Stan back to make sure you get home safe." And then he turned and followed his girlfriend.

"Brother?" Owen asked as they walked away.

I shook my head. "I'm an only child."

"Who's Stan?"

"Our driver for the night." I took a big sip of margarita. "Because if we're going to be the big fun that misses planes, we're going to need a few more shots."

Owen watched me silently for a long moment, making me swallow my nerves. Maybe I'd read him wrong.

"Unless you're not game…"

The corner of his mouth kicked up in a smile, and his eyes settled on my lips. "Oh Little Miss Muffet, I'm definitely game."

3

Pregnancy Week Two and Some Change:

 Who knew you would still
need another lesson on how
to properly use a condom.

Owen

"WHERE ARE WE GOING?" This complex looked awfully familiar, but hadn't we decided on her place?

"Change your mind? Or did you forget we're heading back to my place?" Cece giggled and captured my mouth with hers. Fuck, her lips were soft and full.

Heaven.

And it had been forever, months even, since I'd kissed a woman. Who cared if we lived in the same complex? The car came to a stop, and I released my hold on the back of her neck.

She blinked her somewhat hazy eyes.

How much had she had to drink tonight? Just a couple of shots, right? And a margarita or two.

"Thanks Stan. You're the best," Cece called as she stumbled out of the car.

I caught her waist and pulled her close. Once again, she leaned into me and brushed her lips against mine. I couldn't remember ever wanting someone like this. Was it the liquor? I doubted it. The second this woman had fallen—though it was more like she'd tried to bury herself inside my shirt—I'd been hooked. Every touch we shared was charged. And teasing, flirting, talking had been easy.

"You're good, right?" I asked. I wanted her. I was as hard as a damn brick with need for her. But if she was too drunk, then I'd say goodnight now. I scanned the parking lot, wondering how she'd take it if I bowed out, and my head spun. Whoa. How drunk was *I*?

"Yip, come on." She pulled me by the wrist toward the building. At the door, she messed with her keys. It took a hot minute, but she finally got the door open, and then her irresistible mouth was back on mine.

I had had no intention of stumbling into a sexy blonde's apartment tonight. But I had never been so glad to have a margarita dumped on me. Having my hands on this perfect ass and my mouth devouring the lushest pair of lips I'd ever kissed was more than worth it.

Fuck. I pulled Cece tighter against me when she almost toppled backward over the threshold into her apartment.

Did she trip on something, or were we so drunk that neither of us could walk straight? We'd made it from the car to her door fine. She *did* sort of fall out of the car, but curbs could be tricky like that. They jumped out for no reason.

God bless Stan and his car. But the LA guy—what was his name—

Cece slipped a hand under the hem of my T-shirt, and I fought a shiver as her nails brushed against my skin. It was light, but holy hell, did it make my dick surge against my zipper. I pressed into her, forcing her against the wall, and thrust my hips forward. I was dying to be inside her.

"Can't let the cat out," she mumbled as I trailed my lips down her neck.

Raising my head, I glared at the wall I had her pinned to, only then realizing that it wasn't a wall at all. I had her braced against the open front door.

I stepped back, tugging her with me, and the door slammed shut. Once again, we tripped over something. Shoes? Holy shit, how many people lived here?

"Roommates?" I asked.

"Just Flame and me." Cece breathed, wrapping her arms

around my neck. She tipped her head toward the orange tabby sitting on the arm of the sofa like a statue with its attention locked on us, and its head cocked to the side.

"Cute cat." I ran my hands up under her shirt and pressed my mouth against the soft skin of her neck again.

"He's a demon." A moan slipped past the luscious lips I hadn't been able to take my eyes off all night.

"Bedroom?" I muttered against her skin. I itched to strip us out of our clothes and take her right here, but the room spun again, worse this time. Having a flat surface might help.

She nodded but didn't move or give me direction. The layout was the same as my place on the other side of the complex, so I shuffled toward the bedrooms, pulling her with me.

"I don't normally do this," she said from behind me.

Drunken hookups weren't my go-to either. But unless she said no, walking away now would be impossible.

But even in my drunken state, my subconscious niggled at me. There were words I should say, but I couldn't remember them. Instead, I pulled her close and pressed my lips to hers.

Cece palmed my cock, and my eyes drifted closed. At least I wasn't so drunk I couldn't get it up. Now, though, with the sensations ripping through my body from her touch alone, I was worried I wouldn't last long. Especially once our clothes weren't in the way.

"Need you naked. And on a bed," I sputtered.

Wow. Smooth. Had I lost my touch? Or was I so drunk I couldn't form decent sentences?

The thought left me the second we were inside her bedroom, because Cece's hands went to the hem of her shirt, and she tossed it on the floor.

I stood, frozen in place, staring at her gorgeous tits encased in a lacy nude bra.

The room spun, and I stumbled forward.

Shit.

Too much alcohol, but I didn't care. Getting us both naked was all that mattered.

Cece flicked at something in her cleavage, and her breasts bounced free.

I was awestruck by the sight. Yes. Right. Naked.

"That's the idea." Cece giggled.

Had I said that out loud?

Didn't matter. I fumbled with the button of my jeans and yanked them down, along with my boxer briefs, then hastily discarded my shirt.

Why was she still wearing her skirt? I'd have to correct that, and quickly.

I teetered forward, and then we were falling.

Onto something soft.

The bed. Good.

I crashed my mouth against hers, my tongue darting out to lick and tease. She tasted like a mix of cotton candy and tequila. She gripped my dick, and stars appeared in my periphery.

Couldn't pass out. Not yet.

I positioned myself between her legs and thrust forward. We moaned in unison from the friction, but her panties still had to come off.

I needed to be inside her. Now. Kneeling, I hooked my fingers into the waistband of her skirt and panties, discarding them in one swift move.

Her pussy was slick with arousal as I slid my fingers up and down before circling her clit.

She whimpered my name. And what a perfect sound it was.

Shifting my weight, I rubbed myself along her opening.

"Condom?" she mumbled before throwing her head back and moaning.

Oh hell. Where was my head? Drowning in alcohol, apparently.

"Top drawer. I'm pretty sure there's one in there." Cece pointed to the piece of furniture that sat next to her bed.

Angling over, I opened the drawer and dug around until my fingers landed on a square packet. Quickly, I fumbled with the wrapper and then the condom as the room spun again. This needed to be quick. I could feel myself on the edge of consciousness.

One thrust forward, and I was seated deep within her.

So wet. So tight. Felt so good.

Leaning above her and holding myself up with one arm, I slammed into her over and over. She arched her back, meeting me thrust for thrust, and cried out my name while I continued to drive into her.

"Need you to come," I said, struggling to not come or pass out.

Her pussy clenched, and her inner muscles tightened into a death grip around my cock. Yes. Fucking yes. Her whimpers as she came were the best thing I'd ever heard.

My orgasm barreled through me as my consciousness faded. Two more thrusts, and I was done. My energy sapped, I fell onto the bed next to her and succumbed to blackness.

4

Pregnancy Week Three:

The morning after. You're
clueless that your
little swimmers are racing to
their destination.

Owen

I BROUGHT a hand to my throbbing head and ran my tongue over my dry lips. Shit, it had been a long time since I was this hungover. Hesitantly, I cracked one eye open. The ceiling looked like the one in my bedroom, but the floral scent was out of place. And the sheets felt much softer than the cheap set on my bed.

Where was I?

I swiveled my head to the side, finding a mass of blond hair on the pillow next to me. Piece by piece, the night came back. The way she'd made me laugh at the bar and her lips on me in the car. Images of her under me swamped me. My gut tightened at just the thought of her. I sat up slowly to keep my head from pounding and let the sheet fall to my waist. Beside me on the bed sat the condom from last night.

Had I been so drunk I didn't get up to take care of it? Or was this a second one? Was it even used? I picked it up with two fingers and swung my legs over the side of the bed. Then I pulled my boxer briefs on and headed toward the bathroom.

I tried to fight it, but a stupid smile flooded my face as I inspected the sleeping beauty on the bed. Her hair fanned out on the pillow, and she had one arm tucked under it. Her skin was fair, and in the morning light, I caught the dusting of freckles across the bridge of her nose. They matched the sprinkle across her tits. The white sheet skated across her round breasts, so full and perky. Damn, she had great tits, and long-ass legs that felt exactly right wrapped around my hips. Last night had been a good night.

After two weeks, I was finally earning respect from the guys at the station and settling in with them. Last night had been the second time I'd gone out for drinks with them. But I was glad I'd stayed to finish my beer after they'd all headed out, because meeting Cece had been the highlight of the night. It was exactly what I needed.

And maybe this could become something more than a drunken hookup. I'd love to take her out to dinner. Or to a baseball game.

It had been six months since everything with Tasha had gone to hell, and if I was honest, I'd started pulling away a month or two before that. An almost sixth sense had made me realize she was seeing rings in the future of our relationship, while I wasn't at all. I wasn't opposed to the idea of settling down and white picket fences, but Tasha wasn't the girl I'd do that with when the time came.

I flushed the condom and washed my hands before heading out in search of water. Would making breakfast for her be an overstep?

Before I got two feet down the hall, an orange ball of fluff wrapped around my leg.

My knee cracked as I squatted. "What's your name, buddy?" I got four rubs over the little guy's ears in before the cat batted at me. "Okay, I hear ya. Enough is enough." If this little guy was anything like my parents' cats, he was hungry. Maybe I'd find my food in the kitchen.

I pushed back to my feet, catching sight of a host of pictures cluttering the length of the hallway wall.

I smiled at one of Cece in a cap and gown, but the smile slid from my face when my attention moved to the older man standing next to her in the picture.

I froze.

My eyes widened, and I swore my heart stopped.

No f-ing way.

This couldn't be possible.

The chief's daughter...

The chief's *hands-off* daughter.

No.

I shook my head in utter disbelief. Karma wasn't this cruel.

The bombshell I'd met last night couldn't be my boss's daughter. Frantically, I searched the photos. A few of Cece with her friend from last night. Kelly, maybe? But then another. And another. In three more pictures, it was clear the man in the photo was my chief.

And Cece was too young to be his girlfriend, right? Maybe his sister?

Panic made me stupid. I shook my head. She'd told me she was an only child. And if this was my chief's girlfriend, that would be way worse than his daughter. Maybe. I wasn't actually sure which scenario would be worse...

I took a deep breath, trying to settle myself. Every fiber of my being wanted to flee the house. There was no way I'd gotten myself into something like this again. This time, it had been unintentional, but that didn't matter.

When I'd started dating the police chief's daughter in Richmond, I'd known who she was. But I'd had no clue how badly that would upend everything I'd worked so hard for.

From that experience, I had learned not to shit where I ate.

This couldn't happen *again*.

No way.

But...we'd been pretty drunk. Maybe she wouldn't remember me. That thought made me want to kick my own ass. If she didn't remember me this morning, then I was ten shades of a douchebag for sleeping with her last night. Exactly the kind of guy the chief wouldn't want with his daughter.

I was so screwed. Out of all the people I could have a hot night of drunken sex with...

I had to get out of here. The idea of leaving without waking her made me feel like an asshole, but I had no other choice.

5

Pregnancy Week Six:

Missing a flight out of Florida
was nothing compared to
missing a period.

CeCe

OF ALL THE ways to describe me, late wasn't one of them. I was always on time. Always on schedule. And my cycle wasn't any different.

"Kel—" I blurted the second my friend's face appeared on the phone screen.

"Are you in the supply closet?"

"Yes," I hissed.

Kelly's eyes widened. "The hot nurse?"

"What?" My ponytail fell over my shoulder as I cocked my head. Normally, I was good at following Kelly, but this time, I was lost.

"Did you hook up with that hot guy? Wasn't he a nurse?" Kelly tilted my head, making part of my face disappear. "Or was he the radiology tech?"

"Neither."

"He wasn't a doctor. What does he do? Janitor? Is that why you're in the closet?"

I sighed. If I couldn't rein Kelly in quick, who knew where the conversation would go. "No, I need a favor."

Kelly's eyes widened. "Are you stuck in there? Do you need me to come let you out?"

"I 100 percent did *not* lock myself in the closet, Kelly." I chuckled. That was absolutely something my best friend would have happened to her. "I need you to bring me a pregnancy test."

"The hospital ran out of pregnancy tests? People must be pissed. No wonder you're hiding."

How did Kelly believe that was even a possibility? And did she think one additional pregnancy test would fix a problem like that? But Kelly always spat out the first thing that popped into her head, regardless of whether it made any sense.

I chewed on my lower lip, my stomach flipping at the idea of saying the words that were going to turn my life upside down. "No, *I'm late*," I whispered.

"Late for what?" Kelly's voice was just above a whisper as well.

I threw my hand up in exasperation. "I need a test because I think I'm pregnant," I whisper shouted. "Can you bring me one?"

Kelly's mouth fell open, and her brows pulled together. "Wait—don't they have those there?"

"Yeah, Kel." I sighed again. My friend probably wouldn't follow rules if she were in this situation, but that was one of the many ways we were different. "But we can't use hospital tests and drugs however we want."

"That's dumb. What's the point of being at a place where they have millions of little dip sticks if you can't even use one?" I shook my head. "How late are you? Are you sure you're not just freaking out?"

"Of course I'm freaking out, you nitwit—" I immediately regretted my words when Kelly's eyes widened on the screen.

"No need to be mean."

I took a deep breath and forced my nerves to calm a bit. Because I absolutely didn't want to be a bitch to my bestie.

"I'm sorry, Kel. I'm freaking the hell out because I am so regular I could bet on it. I'm five days late. I swear my heart stopped when my phone beeped a few minutes ago. My period tracking at said I was late and might want to consider a test. I guess I've been too busy to notice. But the app says I've never been more than three days late. Ever. In the history of my cycle." I was supposed to be on the floor, but there was no way I could think until I knew for sure. Hence the reason I was hiding in a closet.

"Of course you've been tracking your period for years. I don't even know what day mine started last month." Kelly rolled my eyes. "Why worry so much about it? It's like one of those things that either happens or it doesn't. Stressing won't make it show up."

I needed to stop this jaunt down a rabbit hole. "Kel, please?"

"I've got you. Just chill until I get there. It's probably just a weird month. New job stress, living alone stress, the demon cat stress. It's been a lot. I'm leaving now. Whatever it is, we'll figure it out. 'Kay?"

"Yeah, okay."

But twenty minutes later, I wasn't any calmer. I was pacing the lobby when Kelly entered through the large sliding automatic doors and practically tackled her once she was inside.

"Did you get it?" I asked as I pulled my friend off to the side and out of sight of the staff and visitors milling about.

"You literally sound like I'm bringing you drugs." Kelly held up the small bag I was holding. "I had no idea if you'd want the ones with all the weird lines or the ones that just say *pregnant* or *not pregnant*. So." She shrugged. "I got them all. I'd want the words. Who wants to add figuring out a code when you're already stressing about whether you're pregnant—"

"I don't care at this point. I just need to know." I yanked the bag from my friend.

"Seriously, chill. Go pee on the stick. You can freak out if there's a problem."

Three tests later, we stood side by side, staring down at the sticks sitting on the edge of the small bathroom sink.

"Well, congrats is definitely not what you want to hear."

Kelly held her arms out, and I stepped into her embrace. I felt like crying while simultaneously choking back the urge to throw up. I'd just started my job at the hospital. How was I going to do this? Although I'd been searching for a new goal to work toward, I'd never imagined motherhood. I worked sixty-hour weeks, and that left little time for me—how would I have time to take care of another person too?

Thank goodness I lived in a two-bedroom apartment, and the second room had been empty since Kelly moved out. But I had Flame. He wasn't even nice to me. What would the demon cat do to a helpless infant? Was I supposed to get my future child on a preschool list now? Was I behind already? I'd never even looked at preschools. I collapsed against the tiled wall beside the sink.

Would I be a horrible mother? I had no idea. My own mother had died when I was little. All that was left of her was a memory of sweet perfume and long blond hair. I didn't know the first thing about being a good mother.

Kelly leaned next to me. "We crawl before we walk," she said, tangling her hand with mine. "You don't need to figure it all out this second, and I'll help."

I dropped my head onto Kelly's shoulder.

"Did you skip the condom?"

"I don't really remember. I found a wrapper the next morning, so I assumed we used one." But I probably needed an STI check, too. How had this become my life?

"Moral of the story: prioritize the depo shot, even if you don't plan on having sex."

"Hindsight is twenty-twenty, isn't it? But I have a bigger problem."

Kelly's shoulder stiffened under my cheek. "What's bigger than being pregnant?"

I let out a long sigh I swore came from deep inside my soul. "Finding the baby's daddy. I have no number, and I don't even know his last name."

"Oh that's not a problem." My best friend relaxed as she waved a hand. "Jack and I will spy patrol that shit up. We can hang out at the bar all week and wait for him. We got you."

I lifted my head and glared at Kelly. "No. That's ridiculous. You can't stalk the bar."

Kelly's lips turned down into a pout. "But it'll be fun. We'll get stakeout snacks and hide in our car until hot baby daddy shows up and then we'll tell him he needs to come with us. You know, like in one of those cop shows we used to watch?"

I shook my head, and despite the train wreck of my life, I chuckled at my bestie's ridiculousness. "That is not the plan." I pulled myself away from the wall. "Right now I have to work, but tonight, I'll figure out how to find him. Half Moon Lake isn't that big."

"Yeah, we could go door to door knocking like Cinderella."

I snorted, but I was too tired to argue with my crazy friend.

By the time I approached my apartment that evening, fatigue had grown into exhaustion. All I wanted was to flop onto the couch with a bowl of ice cream and watch television. Shut off the worries that hadn't stopped all day.

I had no idea how to find the guy I'd slept with. And I still didn't know how I'd raise a child. On top of all that, I was worried about my job. I'd struggled to focus after Kelly left. Twice, I'd zoned out while patients were talking and had to ask them to repeat themselves. Because God forbid, I missed something important like a penicillin allergy. I couldn't lose my job.

This was exactly why I didn't let myself have fun. Fun and I didn't jibe. Fun always caused problems: missed flights, failed tests, accidental pregnancies.

I was preoccupied with the continued doom and gloom when I swung my apartment door open and a blur of fur bolted out between my legs.

No. I didn't have the energy to deal with this. Why couldn't this be one of those few nights where Flame would curl up on my lap? The demon cat had to be at his worst while I was at mine.

I grabbed the treats from the foyer table, but after ten minutes of coaxing, it was apparent Flame was comfy up in his favorite tree. Tears streamed down my face as I stared up at my devil cat.

"Why do you have to be such a pain in the ass?" I whispered to the cat, who stared back unapologetically.

The tree was entirely too high for me to climb, so I had limited options. After the world's longest day, I just wanted someone to take care of it. And I knew just the person.

"Dad?" I choked out, sniffing away my tears.

"What's wrong? Why are you crying?"

"Flame got out. He's up in the tree again, and I can't get him down."

"That damn cat is nothing but trouble. You didn't try to climb up there again, did you? You almost broke your ankle last time."

A week ago, I was halfway up the tree when I got dizzy and fell. I wasn't doing that again. My father was right. I'd been lucky I wasn't hurt.

"No, I didn't try to climb it. I had a crappy day and wanted to curl up on the couch and watch TV. But now I have to worry about this stupid cat who refuses to love me."

A loud sigh came through the phone. "I still don't know what possessed you to get that damn thing."

"I didn't want to be lonely after Kelly moved out. Cuddly cats are supposed to be perfect snuggle buddies." My eyes burned with new tears I didn't entirely understand, but the whole day had been overwhelming.

"Don't cry. Go inside, and I'll send one of the guys over with a ladder. What good is it having a fire chief for a dad if he can't get your cat out of the damn tree?"

I swiped my tears away with the back of my hand. "Okay. Thanks."

Tucking my phone back into my pocket, I headed inside, hopeful the worst of the day was behind me. After all, what else could go wrong?

6

Pregnancy Week Six:

The chief finding out you slept
with his daughter is now the
least of your worries.
Trust me.

Owen

I ONLY HAD an hour left on the clock, and it had been quiet for the last two. A couple guys from the next shift pulled up chairs, and Jay dealt them into our game of rummy.

"Need someone to go help Cece." The chief's command boomed through the large open space of the firehouse.

"Don't tell us it's the damn cat again." Jay huffed and dropped his cards onto the table. "Stupid cliché. Firefighters getting cats out of trees."

"She's crying, so we're going to pretend we like doing this shit." Chief Thompson pinched the bridge of his nose and scanned the group of men.

My chest clenched at the idea of the happy woman I'd met a few weeks ago crying. I wasn't great with tears.

"Wait." Jay spun toward the chief. "Cece's crying? Over the demon cat? Last time I helped her, I didn't think she liked it that much."

"*I* don't like that ball of trouble, but she had a bad day. Now who's turn is it? We've had a good run these last few weeks, but apparently, we're back to getting cats out of trees."

Beside me, Jay mumbled something about daddy's girl.

The chief narrowed my eyes on the young firefighter. "Sounds to me like you're volunteering."

"Nope." Jay nodded at me. "New guy's up."

Oh, no. Hell no.

39

I'd gone out of my way to avoid her—hiding behind bushes, peeking out my curtains, and running to my car like I was being chased by the ghost of Christmas past so she wouldn't spot me. My neighbors all thought I was a hermit because I hardly nodded at anyone before rushing into my apartment every day.

When she turned into the main entrance as I was leaving the other day, I slouched in my seat so low I couldn't see and almost hit the curb, inadvertently drawing attention as the car behind me blew its horn.

What could I say to get out of this? I had to come up with something.

"You're already dressed since you were in the jump car today." Jay tipped his chin at my pants.

Unlike a lot of the guys, I didn't mind being the one ready to go when the alarms rang. Sitting around in my fire pants and boots in an air-conditioned facility wasn't the chore some made it out to be. Plus, I liked being first out and first on scene. But that was coming back to bite me today. Though I swept the room in search of an excuse, I knew there was no way out of this. And maybe, if I was lucky, I could get the cat without having to deal with her.

"McKinley." Chief Thompson's sharp tone rang through my thoughts. "Go, before the stupid thing runs away and we have to spend the next sixteen hours hunting it down."

"Would he do that?" the guy across from me asked.

"Doesn't matter. New guy's got this, right?" Jay smirked. He was a shit stirrer, but I liked him.

I gave a clipped nod and pushed to my feet, ready to face the music. I wasn't sure how mad this woman would be, but my boots felt heavy as I descended the steps and shuffled to the red pickup truck in the garage below. Normally, I got an adrenaline rush when I headed to the jump car, but today, it felt more like I was headed to the firing squad. Odd, since I was usually running into fires rather than doing something as simple as saving a freaking cat.

I ran my hand over my jaw and sighed.

After five weeks, I'd finally settled in with the guys, and although they continued to new guy me from time to time, they listened. And on site, at a fire, no one had any issues with me taking point. Shit. I didn't need that to blow up over personal drama.

Once I was settled in the truck, I ran through the list of ways I could get out of this. But not a single one was reasonable or believable. I'd either have to pass out or puke. If I had a good gag reflex, the puke thing would work, but unfortunately for me, I didn't. It was why I was good at the EMT part of the job. Nothing fazed me. Finding someone lying in a puddle of their own puke? No problem. A bone sticking out of a leg? I didn't react. Gangrene, bed bugs, even leeches were part of the job.

But driving toward the one-night stand I'd snuck out on, who was also my neighbor *and* my boss's daughter, made me want to run for the hills. Best case? She wouldn't remember or recognize me. That would be great. I chuckled darkly, not sure whether I really meant it.

Worst case? New job, new city. Just as I was starting to like this town.

In response to my knock, she swung her front door open, and my heart stopped. Because she looked confused. For a split second, it looked like she didn't recognize me. In the next instant, my stomach sank with dread. Although that had been my best case on the way over, the possibility of it now hurt like a son of a bitch. I needed her to remember.

She was gorgeous. Every bit as beautiful as I remembered. But the paleness of her coloring and the red-rimmed eyes cried out for me to take care of her. And damn it if my knee-jerk reaction wasn't to do just that.

In a heartbeat, her eyes widened.

"Oh my God," she whispered.

I braced myself. Here it came.

"Please tell me Kelly didn't track you down like a stalker. I love her, but I will be arrested for murdering her tonight if she did."

Uh. That wasn't at all what I had expected her to say. I opened my mouth and shut it again. Why would her friend want to track me down? It had been more than a month. Was she still that upset that I'd left without a word? I swallowed hard as Cece gave me a thorough once-over.

She brought her focus back to my face, her expression filled with understanding. "You work for my dad." It was a statement, not a question. "And to think I said this day couldn't get any worse."

Her comment confused me, but at least she wasn't yelling at me for being a douchebag. And the exhaustion on her face and in her posture had me wanting to understand why and wondering how I could make it better. My hand twitched at my side, but I fought the urge to reach out and touch her.

Shit. This wasn't the reaction I was supposed to have.

I was standing here, still not talking, staring almost slack-jawed. *Get it together, idiot.* I cleared my throat. "Your cat?"

She sighed and nodded to the front of the building. "Flame's over there."

I snapped to attention at the word. "There's a fire?" I spun, taking in my surroundings, but nothing seemed to be burning. The air smelled fresh and clear, and there was no heavy cloak of smoke.

"No. *The cat.* I told you his name was Flame. Because he's the devil incarnate."

"Oh." Of course there wasn't a fire. I was here for the cat in a tree.

I turned back to her, and heat flared up my neck. Although I had dark hair, my Irish roots meant I had fair skin that went

42

ruddy with my embarrassment. But I hadn't remembered the cat's name. Had I really been that drunk?

"Sorry. I—uh." I glanced over her head, unable to meet her gaze with the admission. "Some of the details about that night are foggy."

Cece huffed, then brushed past me and strode out to the large tree.

"I'll get the ladder," I said to her back.

I had to apologize to her. She wasn't freaking out on me, but she was upset. And I couldn't blame her. At this point, she probably thought I was a fucking moron.

7

Pregnancy Week Six:

Don't worry. Google says dizzy
spells are a common pregnancy
symptom. But you should verify
that preschool list rumor.

CeCe

OH GOD, I was going to have to tell him. Probably not while he was up on a ladder, though. Hey dude, *I'm pregnant with your baby*, was the type of admission that might have him missing a rung and falling to the ground. With my luck, he'd break his back. He was an asshole who'd slipped out in the middle of the night, but that didn't mean I wanted to kill him. So yeah, now wasn't the time.

Clearly.

Probably not even when he was on solid ground. This wasn't a two-minute convo. He was on shift, and being the child of a firefighter, I knew the alarm might go off at any second. We should meet when he wasn't working. But with as awkward as he was acting, would he even be willing to meet me?

He'd bolted before I woke up, so the message had been received, loud and clear. In any other circumstance, I wouldn't force the guy to talk to me again. We'd had a one-night stand, and I'd willingly signed up for it. Even if waking up to find him gone had stung. Being an adult meant not harping on shit that didn't matter. And until I'd gotten the positive test that afternoon, this guy hadn't mattered.

I jumped at the rattle of the ladder as Owen stepped onto the next rung. It was settled against the tree branch next to Flame. The cat's orange tail flicked, but otherwise, he didn't move.

"Cece." Owen's deep voice sent chills down my spine. The way the man said my name was like the slow burn of tequila making its way through me, flipping my stomach. "Cece, remember, you're holding the ladder."

He grimaced down at me from about three feet above my head.

Shoot.

Right.

Once again, I settled my hand against the warm metal, determined to stay focused. All day, I'd felt like my head was in the clouds. A rapid vibration against my ass had me reaching for my phone, but as I tugged it free from the pocket, it slipped from my fingers and landed with a thud in the grass beside my black ballet flats. Without releasing my hold on the ladder, I bent and scooped it up, then straightened to my full height.

Dark spots filled my vision, and my head swam. Not again. I stumbled closer to the tree trunk and rested my shoulder against it, pinching my eyes closed to fight the wave of vertigo.

"Cece, the ladder?" A beat passed. "Uh—are you okay?"

I forced my eyes open so I could assure him I was fine and steady the ladder for him, but before I could utter a word, movement against the tree bark caught my attention. A scream formed in my throat at the sight of a huge eight-legged creature moving toward my shoulder.

No, no, no. That thing would not get on me.

Pushing off the tree in a panic, I jumped. It was far too big to be a normal spider. Weren't they supposed to be, like, the size of a pinkie nail? This one had to be bigger than a quarter. Was it a mutant spider? That was definitely worse than a normal one. Heart racing, I stumbled back another step, bumping into something. I pushed against it, fleeing the tree and the million-eyed threat.

Owen called from above, but I couldn't hear his words over the blood rushing in my ears.

I yanked back again, and the hard metal against my hip finally gave way, letting me past. The ladder smacked hard to the ground with a loud clang. The sound finally knocked me out of my panic, and my stomach dropped when I realized I'd knocked over the ladder. The ladder Owen had been on.

Quickly, I scanned the ground below the tree, but he was nowhere to be seen.

"What the hell?" he yelled from above.

I tipped my head back to look at the place I'd last seen Flame. And sure enough, Owen was now hanging by his hands from the large branch.

Oops.

Flame jumped down and ran up to my door. Thankfully, I'd left it cracked in case the orange demon wanted to go back inside on his own.

"Can you pick up the ladder, please? I'm stuck."

I eyed the thing lying in the grass. It was awfully close to the tree. Where had the spider gone? How fast could it move?

"Do you know anything about huge mutant spiders?"

"For fuck's sake, a spider again?" he snapped.

"I—" Cringing at his tone, I looked between where he hung from the branch and the ladder. *Be a grown-up*, I chided myself, but my feet didn't move.

He sighed. "Fine."

With more grace than I thought a man his size could possess, he swung his feet over to another branch and worked his tall frame into a crouch. Then he shimmied down to a lower branch, and finally, he landed with a thud in front of me.

Wow. That was hot.

"Are you okay?" Owen asked as he gripped my shoulders.

All I could do was nod as I stared into his dark blue eyes.

"Where's the cat?"

I finally found my voice as Owen broke eye contact and searched for Flame. "He ran back to my apartment."

"Of course he did." He shook his head. "We probably need to talk."

"You have no idea," I mumbled.

"What—" he began, but loud tones coming from his truck rang out in the air.

Owen moved instantly, and I trailed behind him.

"Engine sixteen, truck seven, ambulance twenty-one, respond to a structure fire at 168 Taylor Street. Cross streets Adams and Charles. Repeating..."

Side by side next to the truck, they listened as the dispatcher repeated the call before the beeping tones rang again.

A moment later, my dad's voice came through the radio. "McKinley, jump car needs to get to the scene."

"I gotta go." He spun, pulling his attention from the vehicle to me. "But we'll talk soon."

And from the sincerity in his expression, it didn't seem like an empty promise. It almost looked like he might want to see me again. Though that would probably change after I broke the news to him.

"Okay."

He tossed the ladder on top of his truck and locked it in place before climbing in. He was pulling out before I realized that I still hadn't gotten his number. Again. No phone number, no idea where he lived. At least I knew where he worked.

Oh boy—I winced—my father would probably kill him when he found out. Nerves flipped my stomach at the thought of his reaction. I'd have to wait a little longer to tell Owen. So for now, I should probably figure out whether that preschool rumor was true.

8

Pregnancy Week Six Point Five:

Just so you know, car seats
and cribs are anything but
casual.

Owen

THE RIG BUMPED OVER A POTHOLE, and although the stretcher was locked into place, instinct had me reaching out to steady the man lying beside me. The white sheet was rough on my palm as I pressed down, but the man didn't even flinch. I watched his face, which screamed annoyed rather than suffering. The neck brace was probably overkill, but that didn't matter. Procedure required stabilizing patients after a car accident.

Between the fire that lasted well into the night and the early EMT shift today, exhaustion washed over me in waves. But at least it had been quiet. Besides one refusal of treatment, this was the first call we'd had.

"Five minutes out." The older woman's voice crackled on the radio from the front of the rig. As procedure dictated, I used that time to recheck the patient's vitals for intake. Since this was a low-key, nonemergent transport, we'd secured the patient quickly and were on our way. Other than mild whiplash from the fender bender, it was unlikely the man would have lasting issues. Some first responders fought with adrenaline spikes during calls, but I had always been calm and levelheaded in a crisis. It was part of why I was good at my job.

I entered the guy's vitals into the Twiage app as the rig rounded the final turn toward the hospital. Though this was my first EMT shift since the move, my national EMT certification meant I didn't have to recertify when I moved to Half Moon Lake. Still, not everything was the same. Thankfully, this app was one of the things I had been familiar with when I was at Richmond FD.

It took less than three minutes to get the man out of the back of the bus. And Terri, my counterpart for the shift, led the way into the unknown hospital. The emergency room doors swooshed open, and we pulled up to a desk with a young girl sitting behind it. I began with my normal procedure and only ran into a few bumps as I passed on information and vitals. But my attention shifted when I spotted Cece across the room talking to a nurse.

Both the stethoscope tucked around her neck and her blond braid rested against her bright white lab coat.

She'd mentioned working at the hospital the night we'd met, though I hadn't realized she meant the ER. After yesterday, spotting her here wasn't such an awful surprise.

Cece hadn't mentioned anything to her father as far as I could tell. In fact, Brian had texted me this morning and thanked me for my help. Which made me feel like a jerk, because Brian shouldn't be thanking me for anything when it came to Cece.

I studied her face and gave her a once-over. She was dressed professionally, but all I saw was the swell of her breasts pulling against the green fabric and how the black pants clung to her hips. I sucked in a breath and blinked. My hand twitched like it was desperate to run over every one of her curves.

Damn, even slightly pale and with tired eyes, she was gorgeous. Had she had another bad day? I wanted to apologize for...well, everything I'd done since we met. But now wasn't the time. It had been too late to swing back by her place after we'd gotten the fire out last night. But we still needed to talk.

She glanced my way. Just like the first time we'd locked eyes in the bar, the room faded away. The air buzzed, charged with electricity I was certain she felt too. She didn't turn away. Rather, she watched me as intently as I watched her. I swallowed hard, longing for something I couldn't have. Why did she have to be the chief's daughter?

After a long moment, I pulled my shoulders back, frowning, and finally looked away. After getting the patient setup in room four, I pushed the stretcher toward the doors that would lead back out to the rig.

"Owen?" Cece called, and I turned. "I was wondering if you could come over to my place tonight."

I grimaced. Not because I was opposed to talking to her. I owed her an *I'm sorry for acting like a tool bag* and an explanation about why we couldn't explore whatever hovered between us, but I didn't want to lead her on.

"No." Cece shook her head like she was reading my thoughts, and an enticing blush rose over her neck and cheeks.

My mind flicked back to the same flush weeks ago. It was exactly what happened when she came. A lot of details of that night were hazy, but the image of her face as she fell apart lived rent free in my mind.

I rubbed a hand over my jaw, forcing myself to focus on the right now.

"I just want to talk. And I thought my place would be better than here." She waved a hand in the air.

Right. Head out of the gutter, McKinley. Talking was good. We needed to do that. And the disappointment I felt because she only wanted to talk was ridiculous, but that knowledge didn't stop it from flooding me.

Either way, I dipped my chin. "Sure."

After my shift, I took a quick shower. I'd just tossed on shorts and a T-shirt when my phone rang. The name on the screen had me stopping in my tracks.

Danny.

Although I texted with both of my college roommates regularly, the three of them only ever called in *my back is against the wall, help me* situations. And this wasn't just a call. This was a FaceTime request. There was no scale for rating this kind of thing.

"Dano."

"She's moving back."

Fuck. If that meant what I thought, I didn't have time for this conversation. I had five minutes to get to Cece's apartment, and if I was late, she might pull a Tasha and badmouth me to anyone who would listen. Try to get me fired. Even start a grassroots campaign about how much the lieutenant of the fire department sucked.

I froze. Wow. Those were my first thoughts, and that alone showed me how crazy my ex-girlfriend really was. Cece wouldn't do that just because I was a few minutes late. I'd been an ass since I'd slept with her, and still, she'd been nothing but reasonable. I shook my head and tuned in to the conversation again.

"Glory?" I hedged. The history between my best friend and Glory Demoda spanned years, and the emotional baggage would no doubt require an oversized luggage fee.

"This better be quick." Pete, the last member of the trio, joined the call.

"Glory's moving back to Jersey." Danny's jaw locked, and I glanced away.

Pete blinked twice. "Well...that sucks."

Danny blew out a hard breath. "She's going to be at beer nights, holidays, family dinners. And I—" He ducked his head as his words cut off.

Was the end of that sentence *I don't want to see her*? Or *I don't know if I can stay away from her*? Either way, the way Glory had broken things off with Danny sent a clear message that Danny shouldn't ignore.

Pete met Owen's eyes through the phone screen.

"Listen." I cleared my throat. "Maybe it's time to consider the bureau's offer."

Danny was an arson investigator with the FBI, and they'd been trying to get him to transfer to DC for the last two years.

"I've been thinking that all day," Danny admitted.

"The hell you say?" Pete said. "You can't leave New York. Who will I hang out with?"

Danny scoffed, and I chuckled.

"People don't like me, you assholes."

It was true. Even I hadn't been Pete's biggest fan for the few first months we shared a dorm room during our freshman year. He was direct and often harsh. Even though he had a good heart, he often came across like a self-centered prick.

"You don't need to move; you just need to get over this chick. Find someone to take your mind off her, or better yet"—Pete clapped my hands—"pierce your dick. Women will flock to you. Jacob's ladder is the new thing."

I winced. My entire body rebelled at the idea of a needle in my junk. "*Don't* tell me you did that."

Pete laughed. "I don't need the enhancement. My dick speaks for itself."

God, Pete was an idiot.

Danny's blue eyes narrowed. "You have no idea what it's like to want something you can't have. You want something, you buy it."

Pete snorted and rubbed the scruff on his jaw. "I don't buy women."

Eh. Questionable.

Pete grew up rich, but after his uncle died, he inherited his company, and that elevated him to billionaire status. So, although he didn't *technically* pay for sex, he spent a lot on the women he dated casually. They used him for what he'd buy them, and he used them for blowjobs.

"Dano, I know what it's like to want someone you can't

have." That was an understatement. I hadn't stopped thinking about Cece in weeks.

"Why? Because you have some stick up your ass about your boss's daughter? You want her, and she's clearly interested, but you're letting some nothing issue get in your way." Danny shook his head. "You have no idea. If Glory wanted me, *nothing* would stop me from making her mine." With that, my screen went black.

I winced. Was I making a big deal of nothing? Maybe giving things a try with Cece—

"At least I wasn't the one pissing him off this time." Pete smirked.

I jerked back to the conversation. "Good job."

"No need for the sarcasm. But I agree with Dano. You've been talking about this chick since the night you met her. See where things go instead of stressing about—What?" Pete turned his head. "What do you mean strike?" He glanced back at me. "Later, dick."

And with that, Pete hung up, letting the self-centered prick shine in full force.

I dropped my phone into my shorts pocket and headed to Cece's building. All afternoon, I'd been hoping this would be quick. I'd apologize, and we would agree nothing else could happen between us. But now all I could think about was taking her out, wrapping her in my arms, the feel of her lips against mine.

Cece seemed chill. If it was casual, and I made sure there were no expectations, then maybe...

My brain short-circuited when she answered her door.

"You wear glasses?" I cleared my throat to get rid of the rumble, but damn. Add in the braid she was still sporting, and she had perfected the hot librarian fantasy. Images of her on her knees with nothing on but those glasses flashed through my mind.

"Uh. Yeah." Adorably, her brows pulled together, causing a small line on her otherwise flawless pale skin. Such long lashes. Not to mention the cutest nose.

What. The. Hell? Since when did I think noses could be cute? What was it about this woman that made my thoughts so ridiculous?

"I have to wear them if I don't have contacts in." She nibbled her lip and shifted on her bare feet.

My stomach tightened as I took in the rest of her. Long legs, red toenails. I swallowed. My fantasies had always been about long-legged blondes in glasses. Smart. Sweet. Funny. Cece was all that. And Danny was right; if I played this right, then working with her dad was a nonissue. In that second, all my worry faded. We could absolutely have a casual thing, as long as we were clear on the casual. I just had to apologize and explain. It would be okay.

"Glasses are hot," I assured.

She didn't respond. Only blushed, tucking her hair over her shoulder.

I took a step closer and was hit with a soft, floral scent that was so Cece. The smell brought back flashes of the way her breath hitched when I ghosted my lips over her neck. I fought the groan that wanted to rumble out of my chest.

She stepped back. "Come on in."

My attention snagged on the pile of shoes by the door, then landed on her white lab coat slung over the arm of the sofa as I followed her further into the apartment. The place was cluttered. It wasn't *messy*, but her keys, purse, phone, and a bunch of papers and a notebook sat randomly on the island that separated the kitchen from the living room. A blanket was half draped over the couch. Shoes and light sweaters cluttered the entryway. Unopened mail sat on both end tables.

"I know you didn't really want to come."

My head snapped in her direction. "That's not true. It's just—"

She held out her palm. "I get it. One-night stands end after the night. And I'm not trying to make it awkward."

All this worry about her making things difficult, and we were on the same page. I sighed.

"You're not." I shook my head. "Listen, I got into my own head, thinking you'd expect serious."

Her chin tipped up. "Serious?"

I shrugged. "Sometimes, after a hookup, women become obsessed with picket fences and baby strollers."

She crossed her arms and narrowed her eyes at me.

Fuck. I'd just implied she was the type of nutcase who would sleep with a guy and suddenly start planning a wedding.

"Not that you'd do that. You had no expectations and weren't becoming a clinger."

Clinger? Had I really just said that? I winced.

Cece's lips pulled into a tighter line with every stupid thing I said.

"But it was me being a dick again." I rushed the words out. "I pretty much own the market on being a total tool bag since that night."

Miraculously, her expression softened slightly.

"I walked out of your room and saw a picture of my boss on your wall, and I panicked."

"Owen—"

"So I ran out of the house. Because my last girlfriend was kind of my boss's daughter." If *word vomit* was listed in the dictionary, this would be its definition. They just kept coming. "And she went nutso. And because I wouldn't marry her, she did everything in her power to get me fired and make me seem like an abusive asshole." *Geez, Owen, shut the fuck up.* Even as my brain screamed at me, my mouth kept moving. "So I promised no more shitting where I ate and no more crazy, and then there was you."

That brought a glare to her face. Shit. I'd implied she was crazy.

"Please, God, let me stop talking." With that, I locked my jaw.

Cece barked out a laugh. "Finally, we're thinking the same thing."

I rubbed both hands over my face. "I was messed up, and you got the brunt of it. But I—"

"Owen—"

"—haven't stopped thinking about you—"

"Owen—"

"I really want to try something casual without expectations."

"*Owen, I'm pregnant.*" She slapped her thighs as the frustrated words echoed around the quiet apartment.

I blinked. "You're..." I swallowed.

"Pregnant," she repeated.

Well, that changed...everything.

Speechless, I stared at her as the words sank in. When my knees wobbled, I lowered myself into the plush armchair to my right. Pregnant. Like a kid. My kid. I blinked again.

"I don't have any expectations. If you don't want to be involved, I'm fine doing it on my own, but you have the right to know."

I nodded.

Wait—w*hat*?

She thought I wouldn't want to be *involved*?

"Why would you think I don't want to be involved?" My eyes snapped up to her wide, hazel gaze.

She huffed out a loud sigh. "We did *just* have a conversation about crazy girls and baby strollers, right?"

Shit. Yeah. But...

"That was before."

"Before?" The cute line appeared between her brows again.

"Yes. Before life changed. Before I was going to be a dad." I took a deep breath. Just saying the words felt weird as hell. Me as a dad? I shook my head. Boy, I'd have to call my parents, because I had no idea how to take care of a baby.

Her shoulders relaxed, and she pressed her lips together. "That's it?"

I studied her for a second, wishing I could read her mind. "What?"

"No questions? No paternity test? Nothing?" The words were almost whispered, like saying them might give me an idea.

The honest answer spilled from my lips. "I'm a dick, Cece. From everything I've heard about you, you aren't. I'm betting if you weren't 100 percent sure that baby was mine, we wouldn't be having this conversation." I flopped back into the chair and inspected the ceiling.

"Okay."

I glanced back at her face, seeing her blinking hard.

"Okay," I repeated, though I didn't feel nearly as calm as she looked. Inside, I was panicked, while she seemed like this was any other day. Would it kill her to be less put together?

She nodded and swallowed, then moved to the island in the kitchen and picked up a notebook. "The preschool thing in a small town isn't an issue, so we're good there."

What preschool thing? Like for the bigger small people? The ones without diapers? That was at least a few years away, wasn't it?

"But daycare will be. So we'll have to find one soon."

Soon? Pregnancy was nine months, right?

She held out the notebook to me. "Here are some options."

With a shaky hand, I took the notebook from her and read the list labeled *Daycares*.

She went back to the counter and picked up a stack of

papers. "I made two more lists for cribs and car seats that have the best reviews. I printed out each one so we can compare." She dropped the papers on the coffee table and paced in front of it. "What do you think?"

I should say something. Anything. But what the hell? She'd just broken the news, and now she was handing me lists and wanting me to make decisions? Would it make me an ass if I told her I needed a minute? Maybe we could get our parents' and my older sisters' opinions on this shit.

Oh shit. Her dad was going to murder me. Had she told him already?

"How long have you known?" I asked, looking at the pages of notes.

"I found out yesterday." She froze and swallowed. "But I panicked when I saw you. I should have told you then." She hurried. "But it didn't feel right."

The look in her eyes was pleading. Like she was worried I'd be upset. But I was nothing but confused as hell. She'd only found out yesterday? Does this mean she'd done all this research last night?

"Did you sleep?"

She shook her head. "Turns out telling a guy I'm going to have his baby is nerve-racking as heck." Looking away, she swallowed thickly and shifted from foot to foot.

I dropped the papers on the chair as I stood.

Her eyes tracked me. "And I—"

I cut her off. I wrapped my arms around her and pulled her to my chest. The poor woman was freaking out. My heart stuttered as she leaned into me. This woman was already taking care of the most important thing that might ever exist in my life, so I needed to start taking care of her.

9

Pregnancy Week Six and Half:

Time to get to know your baby daddy.
Yes you totally should have done it
before you saw those two little lines.

CeCe

"HAVE YOU EATEN?" Owen pulled back a little so he could meet my eye.

I blinked and took a breath. He moved so fast. We'd gone from talking about daycares and car seats to being wrapped in a hug and talking about food in a matter of moments.

I *should* be used to that, since Kelly did it to me all the time. But Kelly's thoughts moved more predictably than Owen's. He kept throwing me for a loop.

He ran both hands down over my back one more time, then stepped away. The loss of his warm body and strong embrace was more potent than it should be. We hardly knew each other, so why did I already crave his hug? And why did I feel so relaxed in his arms? Like it would all be okay?

He cleared his throat. "When was the last time you ate something?"

"I had yogurt earlier at the hospital. I'm fine." I waved a hand, brushing off the comment. "We have to make some decisions. We have so much to figure out..."

"Rome wasn't built in a day. Our little guy doesn't need a car seat for another nine months, but he needs nourishment today." He pushed a piece of hair that had escaped from my braid away from my face. The way his finger skated across the curve of my ear sent a shiver down my spine. "Trust me. We have today's problems." A small smile pulled at the corner of his

61

mouth. "Then we have future Owen and Cece problems. Food is a right-now thing. The car seat—damn, I feel sorry for future Owen when he has to read all that shit you printed."

I rolled my eyes but couldn't hold back a chuckle at his teasing smirk. Nothing about this was going how I thought it would. I'd worried that he'd be mad, or that he'd claim it wasn't his. Or panic. But besides the word vomit about his ex when he got there, he'd been calm and a little...perfect?

Owen rounded the island that separated the living area from the kitchen.

Flame stretched and jumped off the sofa. I froze at his movement, forcing myself not to flinch away from the cat that was supposed to be my loving, cuddling buddy. But instead of clawing my leg, Flame pranced off after Owen. He jumped onto the counter, and Owen reached out like he was going to pet him.

"Careful!" I blurted, picturing scratches and blood.

But Owen raised his brow as he stroked the cat's back like it wasn't an impossibility. "Of what?"

I gaped at the purring feline snuggling into his palm. What the hell? The demon cat was like putty in the gorgeous man's hands.

"Uh, Flame is never that nice."

Owen shrugged. "He seems like a softy to me. Right little man." Owen smiled and lifted his other hand to pet him.

Flame brought his paw up and batted gently at Owen, who pulled away.

Of course he'd charmed my evil cat. From the beginning, he had charmed me too.

Owen turned away from the counter and opened the fridge. Immediately, he frowned at me over his shoulder, his blue eyes piercing into me. "You have no food in here. Just orange juice, water, and milk. What do you eat?"

I spent so much time at the hospital these days that most of my food rotted in my fridge. The third time I'd gagged at a spoiled bell pepper and moldy cheese, I stopped buying it.

"I usually just grab something at the hospital."

"Let's go to my place." He shut the fridge door and straightened. "It's a short walk, and I have a fully stocked fridge. I can whip us up something quick."

Walk?

My eyes narrowed. "When you say a short walk…?"

He chuckled and rubbed his jaw, suddenly unwilling to meet my gaze. "I live in the next building over."

"You live *here*?" I couldn't keep the exasperated shock out of my voice. I shook my head. "How have we not run into each other?"

Owen smirked, finally looking away from the very interesting countertop. "Very purposefully."

"Oh my gosh." I barked out a laugh. No way. Was he the sketchy new neighbor everyone was saying must be in witness protection?

"What?"

I shook my head and grinned, "You're the guy who doesn't meet anyone's eye and runs into his house like his hair is on fire."

He ran his tongue over his teeth, and a slight blush rose up his neck. "I hit the curb and almost blew a tire too, just to make sure you didn't see me when you drove past."

I laughed. "You went through a lot of effort to stay away. I should probably be insulted by how hard you tried to avoid me."

Owen's smile dropped from his face, and he took three steps around the island. When he was standing close, he cupped the back of my neck and pulled me closer.

"Please don't be." His deep blue eyes bored into mine as he brushed his thumb against my cheek.

My stomach flipped over at the tenderness of the action, and my breath caught in my throat.

"You are amazing. I'm the world's biggest dipshit. Please don't doubt yourself."

I swallowed at the intensity of his words, and my heart pounded at his proximity. He was mere inches away. The heat of his palm warmed my neck. I wanted to lean in closer.

His gazed dropped to my mouth for an instant, but in a blink, he locked eyes with me again. The warmth of his touch fell away then, as he dropped his hand and stepped back.

"Come on. I want to make dinner to apologize for getting us off on the worst foot ever."

The way he shifted on his feet and the ruddy color still staining his neck implied that he was nervous. Like he wanted me to say yes. After the way he'd run out on me without a good-bye, I had expected tonight to go horribly. But none of it had. Owen was going to be the father of my child, so maybe getting to know him better wasn't the worst idea.

"Fine." I smiled. "Take me to your place."

A person's home said a lot about them.

"Why does that sound like a challenge?" Owen propped an arm up on the counter and tipped his head to the side as he studied me.

"No reason." I spun, going for the door. But a wave of vertigo hit me mid-turn. I flung my hand out to steady myself.

"Whoa." Owen steadied me, his light teasing gone and little lines of concern appearing at the corners of his eyes as he assessed me. "You okay?"

This was becoming ridiculous. How many dizzy spells had I had lately? Seven? Eight? Was it a pregnancy thing?

"Yeah." I nodded.

Although he didn't question further, he didn't let go of my hand the entire walk over to his place.

Ten minutes later I was sitting at his island with a bottle of water, watching him cook dinner in a kitchen that was identical to my own—apart from two big things. One, he had food—quite a bit for someone who lived alone. And two, there was no clutter. Everything had a place. It wasn't empty. Even though he'd just moved in his place was homey and warm. Like he'd lived there for years. He even had a fruit bowl filled with apples, oranges and bananas on his island.

What guy had a fruit bowl? And hand towels? Picture frames, a throw blanket. There was even a plant sitting by the window. I couldn't have plants. Flame either knocked them over or ate them.

"It's a Christmas cactus." Owen said, as if reading my mind. "Although it didn't get the memo about Christmas. The thing blooms whenever it wants." He chuckled. His laugh echoed through me, relaxing me. I liked the sound of it. And that realization made me flush.

I turned away to hide my reaction. Noting the other items on the countertops. The canister for the coffee matched the mugs hanging from little hooks under the counter.

Owen sighed. "I have a mother and two sisters who love decorating. When I lived in Richmond, they all lived a few blocks away. Every time I came home from a twenty-four-hour shift at the firehouse, my house had more stuff." He dropped a handful of vegetables into the chicken he was sauteing. "I'd say I hated it"—he lifted a shoulder and dropped it quickly—"but that would be a lie. As annoying as they can be, I do like to feel homey at home. And they made sure I wasn't living in an empty box."

I chuckled. "Didn't realize you would need hand towels?"

Owen glanced over his shoulder and laughed. "I didn't know I needed a lot of things. I never would have bought myself this Pampered Chef spatula, but now I don't think I could live without it."

I laughed. "You're close with your family."

He nodded and turned back to his sauté pan. "They weren't thrilled when I left the area." He opened one of the white cabinets and pulled out an orange pouch of rice.

That gave me pause. "Will you go back?" I dropped my hand to my lower stomach. If he did, what would that mean for our child?

He put the rice pouch in the microwave and turned to me, swallowing thickly. "I left because I needed a fresh start. Family is important to me, but Richmond isn't my place anymore."

"Because of your ex?" The word vomit had been a lot to take in when I was stressing about telling him I was pregnant, but I'd gotten the general idea of what he had been saying.

As he plated their food, he explained. "I don't want to say I'm blameless, but I knew pretty quickly it wasn't a long-term deal between Tasha and me, so I should have ended it after a few weeks, not after six months. But I thought we agreed to be exclusive, but more casual."

He pushed the chicken stir-fry sitting on top of the bed of white rice across to me. God, it smelled delicious. I hadn't realized how hungry I was until the plate sat in front of me.

"When she started hinting about her lease ending and moving in together, it dawned on me that we weren't on the same page." He handed me a fork and sat on the backless stool next to me at the granite island.

"She didn't take it well?" I scooped up a bite and sighed in bliss. Damn, the man could cook.

"Ha! Not taking it well was an understatement." Owen shook his head. "She said I was unfit to serve at the fire department because of my manic moods. She claimed I had a temper, and—" He gritted his teeth and dropped his fork onto his plate. After a moment, he let out a breath. "She claimed I put my hands on her."

I froze with a second bite halfway to my mouth and turned to look at him.

His eyes pleading. "I swear to God the only time I ever put my hand on her…"

I watched him carefully as he pressed his lips together and studied his plate. The expression on his face was open, sincere.

"I'm not opposed to consensual spanking in the bedroom."

Oh.

Oh.

That thought rocketed through me and settled deep in my core. I took in his hands where they rested on the countertop and pictured them on me. The sting of a good swat on my ass.

My breathing sped up.

"Sorry if saying that is inappropriate. I'm not sure what is allowed with the woman carrying my child." He swallowed.

"Your hands have been on my ass, so I think it's okay." My words were breathless.

His eyes dilated as his gaze dropped back to my mouth. "And what a great ass it is." He glanced away quickly. "Everything Tasha said was bullshit, but it put doubts out there. And truthfully, it became bigger than how well I did my job. I'd spent years working to get myself in a position where I could one day take over as chief, but she ensured that was an impossibility. She wanted the ring, and I wanted the job. I didn't give her the dream, so she took mine away."

He shrugged like it didn't matter. But his grip on his fork was tight as he lifted a bite to his mouth.

"I'm sorry."

He turned back to me. "Why?"

"That wasn't fair to you, and I'm sorry you got the short end of the stick. I've had relationships end before and although it wasn't always what I wanted, I'm wise enough to know that I can't make someone love me. Someone should have taught Tasha that."

Owen examined me, frowning. *Had I said something wrong?* Finally, he nodded.

"Thanks." He turned back to his plate and took another bite of his food. "Anyway," he added once he swallowed. "Now I'm focusing on staying drama free. Do a good job, win the respect of my team, and hopefully I'll move up here. So no, Cece. I don't plan on leaving."

"Sorry I ruined your drama free plans."

He knocked on the counter. "I don't plan to make this drama if you don't."

"No." I shook my head. "I definitely don't."

"Good."

"But I'm not ready to tell my dad yet either."

"Okay." Owen turned back to his food.

"That's it?" I thought he'd insist or say he planned to tell my father. Or that he wanted to be there when I did. Especially after the Tasha story.

He sighed and covered my hand, clinging tightly to my fork with his. "Cece, you're driving this bus. Right now, you're doing all the heavy lifting. You tell me you're not ready to tell people after knowing for twenty-four hours. Good, I respect that. I get it. Just eat. We'll worry about tomorrow's shit tomorrow."

10

Pregnancy Week Seven:

Alcohol is not the only thing you'll
have to avoid during pregnancy.
Your favorite sushi and that
cheese you love are also on the list.

Owen

IT HAD BEEN a week since Cece dropped the news on me, and although she hadn't wanted to tell her dad, she wasn't opposed to me sharing the news with my family.

Weirdest conversation of my life. Grandkids were something my parents celebrated, but there was the *you've only been in North Carolina for two months* part of it. And when my mother desperately wanted to drive down and meet Cece, I had to slow her down and explain that I was still trying to get to know her.

It sucked telling my mom, *hey, I'm personally acquainted with her vagina, but I'm still learning about her heart, head, and personality.*

I winced thinking about it even now.

Both my sisters wanted assurance that Cece wasn't another Tasha. Understandable. But all it took was one conversation. Cece's response to the Tasha story was all it took for both women to come around to the idea of her.

Not only did Cece not question my story or doubt me, but she *understood.* That was a nice change that pulled weird on my chest.

With their worry about Cece put aside, they, naturally, picked like hens, constantly calling and texting me with reminders about what I should be doing for the woman who was carrying my child.

This morning's thing was *what do you mean she has a cat?*

I hadn't known it was dangerous for pregnant women to clean litter boxes. But now that my sisters had read me the riot act, I'd take over that task. I was doing my best where she was concerned. My entire focus, apart from work, was on trying to make life easier for her. She wanted to be independent, but in the end, she didn't really push back against my efforts. It was nice. Even having a meal and a conversation was different. Refreshing. Easy in comparison to the work it had always been with women in the past.

We'd fallen into a friendship immediately and naturally. Our child would tie us together forever, and that meant we needed to have a good relationship. So even though I'd been interested in the hot blonde as a casual fuck buddy just last week, my interest now was in becoming her best friend. My brain understood it, though my dick was still coming to terms with the idea. Because that asshole liked her a bit too much.

I maneuvered my car through the apartment building's parking lot, my attention latching on to the woman who still haunted my fantasies.

What the hell was she doing?

I parked my car, then hustled to her. Hands on her knees, she was bending forward, that perfect ass highlighted in teeny-tiny shorts. I equally wanted to toss a blanket over her and tell any wandering eyes to get the hell away and toss her over my shoulder and take her somewhere I could remove the shorts for a closer look at what was hidden underneath.

I shook my head, pushing away the thoughts.

"Cece?"

"What the—" She jerked up. "Shoot." Her hand shot out in search of something to brace against.

Quick on my feet, I wrapped an arm around her as she swayed sideways. The warmth of her body pressed into me.

"I got you." I tightened my grip, relishing the feel of the

strip of bare skin between her shorts and tank top. She closed her eyes and laid her head against my shoulder. I'd seen dizzy spells enough to know what one looked like. And thinking back, this wasn't the first I'd witnessed from her. How often was this happening? "Okay to walk? You need to get home and lie down."

"I went to take the trash out, but Flame bolted," she mumbled into my chest. Her breath skated across my neck.

Goose bumps broke out on my skin, and I fought the shiver. God, this woman would be the death of me.

I glanced back at the bush she'd been looking under. "Let me get you back to the apartment, and then I'll come back out for Flame."

She nodded. Once I was back outside, it only took five minutes to get Flame to come to me. Although Cece complained about the cat, he was a sweetheart. He had bolted out of the bush and straight into my arm when I'd returned with a package of cat treats.

"Have you eaten?" I asked once I brought Flame inside.

A loud sigh echoed through the room. "Yes. You brought me food at lunch, even though you were on shift."

I had been moving a patient from the hospital to long-term care, so I'd been at the hospital anyway. I'd packed up a lunch at the station and brought it with me. Had Terri given me the side-eye when I put a Tupperware container of stew in the cab with me? Yup. Did I care? Nope.

"And you stocked my kitchen this week, plus you text me three times a day. So yeah. I'm eating."

It wasn't a lack of food.

"Are you drinking all your water?"

Now she rolled her eyes and pointed to the clear almost empty bottle on the coffee table. The water was just below *Good Job!* so if she'd filled it this morning, that meant she'd gotten sixty-four ounces already.

"It's hard to ignore the stupid smart water bottle that sends my phone messages to remind me to drink my water and yells at me when I don't."

What? It's a good invention. Makes sure people are taking care of themselves. It wasn't like I'd hooked it up to my phone to monitor her. I wasn't crazy.

"Good. But we should probably bring the dizzy spells up to the doctor next week."

A slight nod was her only response.

"The appointment is Tuesday, right?"

"Yeah." She swallowed. "You're still coming?"

"I told you we'd go together." I raised my brows at her. "Unless you changed your mind and don't want me there."

That would suck. I wanted to be a part of this baby making thing, and she was nervous and could use my support. But if she said she wanted to do it alone, I'd respect her wish.

"You can come to any you want." She picked at the couch, not making eye contact.

"Cece," I called, but she didn't look up. "Cece," I tried again, and she finally met my gaze. "I want to be at all of them. I want to be there for you, and I want to be there for our little guy."

She almost smiled. "It could be a girl."

"Yeah." I shrugged. "I have a feeling it's a boy, though."

"Me too." She actually smiled this time. "Do you have plans tonight that I'm keeping you from?"

"A date with Flame's litter box." I surveyed the open area, racking my brain for where I'd seen it in the handful of times I'd been here. "You don't happen to have one of those self-cleaning ones, do you?"

"What? No." She sat up and shook her head. "I don't need more smart stuff. I'm perfectly capable of scooping a litter box."

Not anymore. "Where is it?"

Her brows pulled together. "Bathroom."

After cursing to myself, I stepped back into the living room. "It's clean."

"Of course it is. I do it every day—" Her eyes went wide, and her mouth formed an *O*. "Shoot. I can't. And I know better. Oh my God, what else have I forgotten about? I think I had feta cheese on my Greek salad at lunch yesterday. What about cleaning supplies?" She pushed up from the couch. "I should do some research and find out which ones I shouldn't use. Bleach is one I should throw out, and..."

She scanned the kitchen, probably cataloging all the things she could no longer do, eat, or be around. Probably to the extreme.

I'd be the voice of reason. I stepped in front of her and placed my hands on her shoulders. "Cece, stop. Look at me."

Her wide gaze met mine. "I can't believe I didn't think of any of this. I should write myself a list of things to remember to avoid."

I bit back a smile and kneaded the tight muscles under my hands. "Take a deep breath. From now on, I'll clean the litter box. But you don't need to throw out your cleaning supplies. The important thing is to not breathe in the harmful chemicals. Diluted bleach or mild cleaners will be fine. Isn't that what you would tell a pregnant patient in the ER?"

"Yes, but they usually don't know better. I do." She sighed. "I—I don't know what I'm doing. I just want to be a good mom."

She collapsed into me, and I tightened my arms around her. I hated that she was panicking, but I loved having her in my arms. There was something peaceful about holding her.

"You will be."

She shook her head. "Sometimes I feel like I'm missing the tools, because I didn't have the opportunity to learn from my mom."

That's right. The chief was a widower. "How old were you when your mom died?"

"Three. It was always just Dad and me. His parents lived far away, and we hardly saw them." Cece shook her head against my shoulder, pressing her nose into him. "What if I'm bad at momming?"

"Cece, I don't know Brian that well, but he seems like a damn good dad."

"He is."

"So you know how to be a parent. Mom, dad. It's all about loving your kid. You don't have to worry because even I can tell you already love ours."

Her breath hitched and she sniffed.

Shit. Was I making her cry?

"I'm sorry. Did I say something wrong?"

"No." She shook her head but sniffed twice, and I was certain I could feel damp tears on my shirt. "It was perfect."

"Then why are you crying?" I asked.

"I don't know." She half laughed and half sobbed.

Mood swings. Maggie and Shannon had both mentioned those. They were normal. I would roll with this.

"How about I put a movie on? We can just chill."

She lifted her head and sent me a small smile. "Can we make popcorn? I've been craving it all week. Such a weird thing to crave, isn't it?"

"Who doesn't love popcorn?" I smirked. "You don't happen to have M&M's, do you?"

"Um—I don't think so. Why?"

"I like adding them to my popcorn."

"That's weird."

"Don't knock it till you try it."

An hour into the movie, Cece's head was resting on my chest, and her breathing had evened out. Was my arm falling asleep? Definitely. Did I plan on moving her? Nope.

11

Pregnancy Week Eight:

You haven't decided if
experiencing minimal morning
sickness but massive pregnancy
brain is a win or a loss...

CeCe

I FIDGETED with the hem of my blouse. "Really, I'm fine, Kelly. Owen's going to be here any minute."

"The first doctor's appointment is a big deal, so if you need extra backup or just want me instead, you know I got you," my best friend assured.

I appreciated it. And truthfully, I was nervous about Owen being there. It was weird going to the OBGYN with my one-night stand. But he'd spent the last two weeks doing everything he could to help. So how could I tell him not to come?

"He wants to go. He's really trying to do the right thing with all this."

"As he should be. He was there for the fun part, after all."

"I don't think either of us really remembers the 'fun' part."

At least I didn't. Flashes of it. His body pressing me into the door. His fingertips running along my sides. The rough scrape of his stubble against my neck. My legs wrapped around his hips as he moved inside me.

I swallowed as my core once again tightened with the memory. I tried to lock those thoughts away where I wouldn't harp on them. We hadn't had the 'we need to keep this platonic' conversation, but regardless, we seemed to be on the same page with it.

"Cece?"

"Sorry, Kel, I should probably go. Owen will be here any minute."

I was barely off the call when the knock echoed around my apartment. Pulling the door open, I took in the polo, khakis, and Sperrys. Had he dressed up for the doctor? Not that he looked bad. In fact, he looked far from it. The navy fabric clung to his shoulders before draping over his chest and flat stomach.

Once again, I was taken back to the feel of his hard body pressed against mine. The way he'd cupped the back of my head as he dominated my mouth. Owen had mastered the art of kissing. A nip, a tease, then an all-out invasion, taking over my every thought.

"Cece?"

I blinked at the man standing at my door with a white and green to-go cup in his hand. Shoot, how long had I been zoned out? I felt like I was in a fog lately.

"You good?" He cocked his head to the side and frowned.

I cleared the lump in my throat. "Yeah, let's go."

He gave me a once-over. "You're *ready*?" The question turned up at the end like he had expected me to be late.

I wasn't late. That was fact. The sky was blue, the grass was green, and I was always on time. Facts. I'd been waiting for at least twenty minutes for him. Judging by the white cup in his hands, he'd gotten himself coffee before coming to my place.

"Yeah. Just need to grab my purse and phone."

He frowned, and his lips parted. But quickly, he locked his jaw.

"Are you having second thoughts about going?" I asked.

"No." He shook his head violently. "Not at all. I just—" He swallowed. "As long as you're comfortable, it's all good. No matter what."

Why was he acting so weird? Was it nerves? I was certainly nervous, so I could understand that.

"I want you as involved as you want to be," I assured again. Then I waved him in before Flame could escape.

I picked up my purse and snagged my phone from where I'd left it on the counter. When I reached back to slide my phone into my pocket, though, I was met with soft satin rather than my denim skirt. My heart lurched, and I spun to him.

"Were you not going to tell me?"

He blinked twice. "I thought..." His focus darted around the room rapidly like he was searching for an escape. "Well, I didn't want you to feel"—he shrugged but smirked at the same time—"you know. Judged."

"I'm still in my *pajamas*," I screeched. I deserved to be judged. Not for wearing sleep shorts, but because I'd thought I was fully *dressed*.

"Yes." His attention dropped to my legs. "Tiny little shorts." He looked away. "I didn't know if your clothes didn't fit, or if you're one of those people who likes being out in PJs."

"I'm not." I let my arms fall to my sides. I was the kind of person who was always put together. At least I used to be. But now my head was constantly in the clouds, so maybe I was that type of person. Hell, a moment ago, I had been ready to leave the house this way without even realizing it. "I'm getting changed."

I made it to the bed before dropping my head in my hands.

"So what if I'm losing my mind?" I mumbled. "So what if life is off the rails? Who needs a plan? Not me." I tried to convince myself. What did it matter if I was pregnant and not sure I could mom? So what if I wore PJs to the doctor? So what if some guy I hardly knew was going to watch me have an internal ultrasound?

My eyes stung.

"Can I come in?"

I startled at the sound of his voice. Owen was standing in the doorway. The *open* doorway. Hadn't I shut it behind me?

I wiped at my cheeks. Geez, this man didn't need to see me cry again. I nodded, and he moved to the bed to sit next to me, his white Starbucks cup still in his hand.

"Would it help if I promise to always let you know if you're in PJs or if your shoes don't match?"

My eyes widened. "Oh my God, is that a *thing*?"

"No." His answer was too quick to be believable.

I frowned.

"Well." He shrugged sheepishly. "Maybe. Maggie, my oldest sister, by the time she was almost ready to pop, her stomach was so big, she never cared about whether her shoes matched."

I blew out a big breath and eyed him in my periphery. "So I'm going to end up the size of a whale and look homeless and you'll be all"—I waved my hand—"put together and perfect."

He chuckled. "I'll wear two different shoes if you want."

Now it was my turn to laugh.

"And Cece." He turned to look me in the eye. "I'd love to come in and talk to the doctor with you. See the ultrasound of our little guy and hold your hand when you're feeling freaked out just to show you I'm there."

I opened my mouth, ready to agree, but Owen went on.

"But I get that this is awkward. So I'm equally willing to sit in the waiting room and wait for you to show me the picture of the little guy when you're done. I was trying to be supportive, but I'll understand if you don't want me there while you're stuck in a paper shirt with a huge condom-covered wand coated in goo shoved all up inside you."

I scoffed, or maybe it was a gasp. Either way, a weird noise definitely came out of my mouth. It wasn't the words that shocked me. No, it was his knowledge. He knew what to expect. Although I didn't say anything, a slight flush crept up Owen's neck, turning his cheeks a light pink.

He cleared his throat. "I may have asked my sisters what to expect. And then I googled shit so I wouldn't look like a dumb-ass. But I didn't mean to make this more pressure for you. Clearly, I'm fucking it all up."

My eyes narrowed, and I tipped my head. "Oh. I said that all out loud a minute ago, huh?"

Great. But before I could say anything, my stomach rolled. I covered my mouth, swallowing fiercely.

I would not puke. I hated to puke. Luckily, I hadn't had horrendous morning sickness. But in the last week or so, there'd been times that my stomach just felt...rolly.

"You okay?" he asked, shoving the white cup at me. "Here."

I shook my head.

He held it higher. "Medicine ball tea. You said it was the only thing that had been settling your stomach."

Seriously? He'd remembered that?

I took the cup and brought it to my lips. Just the smell of the mint and citrus helped settle me as I took a sip.

Beside me, Owen was studying me, searching. Probably trying to see what else he could do. But honestly, what else could I ask for in a baby daddy? He cared about my feelings, was constantly helping. And even remembered the details. I took another small sip, already feeling better, then tilted toward him and pressed my lips lightly against his cheek.

He froze, and I pulled back.

"Owen, you've been perfect. Thank you. Let me get some pants on, and we'll go see this little man, okay?"

An hour later, even sitting in a paper gown with my feet in stirrups, I was glad Owen was there.

"See that little thing right there?" The doctor pointed at the screen.

My heart lurched, and my eyes flooded with tears.

"That's our little guy?" Owen asked as he gave my hand a squeeze.

I dragged my gaze from the screen so I could look at the

man sitting next to me. He was focused on the little blob of a baby like it was the most amazing thing in the world.

"And this"—the doctor hit a button, and a thumping whoosh echoed around us—"is the heartbeat." Hearing the heartbeat and seeing my baby on the screen was almost over-whelming.

Owen glanced down at me. "I know this probably sounds dumb to you since you're living this, but it feels really real all of a sudden."

I nodded. "I get it."

A small smile touched his lips, and he squeezed my hand again. It was odd how we already felt like a team. Like we were really in this together. I had always planned to have kids. One day, when my career was settled and I'd been married for a few years. Never had I imagined being a single mom at twenty-five. But at the moment, with Owen standing beside me, it didn't seem as scary as it had this morning.

"Everything looks great. Baby and mommy are both healthy." The doctor shut off the machine and handed me a picture. "Do you have any questions for me?"

I blinked rapidly and ran through the million questions I had. I glanced at Owen, unsure of where to start.

"Should we be concerned about the things I exposed myself to before finding out I was pregnant? Like cleaning the cat's litter box or eating lunch meat or soft cheese or the wine I had a few weeks ago?" he asked calmly.

"No." Dr. Wilson smiled. "Obviously, now that you know, you should be careful of those types of things, but don't stress about what you did before you knew you were pregnant."

My shoulders relaxed, and my mind cleared a bit with the relief. I asked a few more questions, and when I'd run out, Owen took over again.

"How common is dizziness? She's been having dizzy spells recently. Is that something we should worry about?"

"It's not completely uncommon." The doctor studied my chart before finally looking up. "Have you always had low blood pressure?"

"Yeah, I'm usually on the low side of average."

"It's probably nothing to worry about. As the blood vessels widen in your body to allow for better flow to you and the baby, it can sometimes decrease your blood pressure. Dizziness and lightheadedness can be a symptom. Make sure you're eating and drinking every couple of hours and stay off your feet when you can."

"Wait." I held up my hand.

"I know that's not always possible with working at the hospital. But when you get the chance, rest and prop your feet up."

I nodded, nibbling my lower lip. How would I manage that? What happened when I got further along? What if I had to go on bed rest? Would I lose my job? What about when the baby was born? How long could I take off work?

Owen squeezed my hand and whispered in my ear. "Rome wasn't built in a day. We'll figure out how later will work *later*. We've got this."

And when he pressed his lips against the side of my head, I desperately wanted to believe him.

12

Pregnancy Week Nine:

Most people decide to tell friends and
family between eight and twelve weeks.
There's no advice for when you knock up
your boss's daughter though.

Owen

I KNOCKED LIGHTLY on the counter, causing Claire's head to
snap up.

A smile slowly took over her face. "Back again?"

I'd just finished up a forty-eight-hour shift with the EMTs,
and I'd been back and forth to this hospital at least fifteen times.
And this woman I now knew was a regular at the intake desk.

"Whatcha bring her?" She eyed the bag I placed in front
of her.

"Dinner." Just leftover ziti that we'd eaten at the station. I'd
learned Cece's routines over the last couple of weeks and knew
that when she worked overnight, she tended to skip dinner.

She sighed and rolled her eyes. "I always ask for specifics,
and you're always so boringly general."

I chuckled. "Is Cece around?"

"Give me a sec. She'll usually come over for you." The
young woman pushed back from the desk and stood.

I pulled my shoulders back and rolled them, giving my back
a good crack.

A moment later, the women appeared.

"It is with the greatest pleasure that the hospital presents"—
the young woman flung her arms dramatically toward Cece—
"your girlfriend."

The words pulled weird at my chest. Almost like I wished
they were true. But did I?

"Friend, Claire," Cece corrected.

Claire scoffed like Cece was an idiot, then spun and walked away.

"I'd ask what brings you by, but I'm good at learning patterns. So, what's for dinner?"

I couldn't fight the smile at her words. "Ziti."

"The Irishman making the Italian food." She peeked into the bag. "God, it smells good."

"It's just from the station."

Her hazel eyes snapped up to meet mine. "Dad told me you do all the cooking there now. He jokes about you being his private chef."

I'd been surprised to realize that none of the guys could cook. Even the EMTs brought food or ordered on shift. In Richmond, we had taken turns making dinner, so I more than knew my way around the kitchen. And everyone at Half Moon Lake FD was thrilled when I was on shift.

I opened my mouth to respond but was overtaken by a yawn.

"You should go home. It's supposed to start storming soon. Going to be pretty bad until, like, noon tomorrow. I knew I should have gotten gas on the way in. It'll suck having to stop in the rain tomorrow morning."

My shoulders tightened, and I knocked twice on the counter between us. The last thing I wanted was the mother of my child pumping gas in the massive thunderstorms coming our way.

"Get me your keys."

Her brows pulled together.

"I'll fill up your tank before I head out. Then you can stay out of the storm."

"You don't—"

"I know I don't have to," I cut her off, "but I want to."

Her lips pulled down, and she remained behind the desk.

"It's my way of helping you and the little guy."

She nodded, then pulled a key fob from the pocket of her white coat. I had to fight the shiver that raced up my arm as her fingers brushed against my palm when she dropped the key into it.

"I'll leave the key with Claire." I didn't want to bother her again. "Have a good night."

"You too." The small smile she sent my way kept me warm, even as I pumped gas in the rain.

"We have a council meeting next week. I'd really like you to come." The chair creaked as Brian tipped back, blocking the bright ray of sun beating in through the windows behind his desk. The view of downtown Half Moon Lake was quaint. The street was lined with little shops and ended with the large park that families and runners regularly frequented.

The first few weeks I was there, I'd pictured a dog in my future, the two of us hanging out in the grass next summer. But now, thoughts of Cece and our little guy hanging out in the grass filled my mind and left me smiling.

"You're not on call here, but are you riding?" Brian asked.

"I'm not on the EMT schedule either on Tuesday, so I'll be there," I agreed.

I'd just walked in for my shift when Brian called me into the office. After a dull thirty-six hours off, I was glad to be back on call for the next seven, but picking up this partial shift maxed out my "on" time for the week.

It might seem nuts working as much as I had the past few weeks, but I wanted to put in extra time now while I could. Once the baby came, I didn't envision myself picking up additional shifts often.

"You're fitting in, kid." Brian smiled.

I gave him a quick chin tilt. "Thanks. I'm enjoying it. You've got a great setup here, and the guys have been great."

"Especially since you cook." He chuckled.

I rolled my eyes. "Yeah. That's become a thing."

"We need to talk about gear replacement. And then I want to go over the guys who are completing training. We can talk about who we want to pick up."

"Sounds good. When?"

"How about we grab a beer and food before the meeting? Get all our ducks in a row."

I swallowed. Brian and I had been getting along great. We worked well together, and Brian listened to my suggestions and advice. Working closely with the chief and being mentored by him was exactly what I wanted. But dinner and beer felt shitty when I was keeping a secret from the man.

"Am I not cool enough to have a beer with?" Brian tilted his head. "I know you do it with the guys."

"I actually haven't for a couple weeks," I muttered.

Brian's brows pulled together, and his lips turned down. "Is something going on? I thought you were fitting in with them."

Shit. I hadn't meant to stir up questions. "No." I cleared my throat. "Just some home stuff. Like being at home. You know stuff. Good stuff. Home."

Wow, good words there.

I tried hard not to squirm under the chief's scrutiny. I respected that Cece wanted to tell her dad in her own time, but with every day that went by, I felt worse about hiding the truth.

"It's good though. Want to burger with you," I blurted.

Want to burger with you? What the hell? Geeze, get it together.

Across from me, Brian was trying not to laugh. "You want a burger. Okay." He shook his head. "We'll get you one. Let's meet at The Dock at five."

"Sounds good." I stood and rushed out of the office. Once I cleared the door, I pulled out my phone.

Me: We need to tell your father. This shit is getting weird.

Cece: What happened?

Me: I just forgot how the English language works and sounded like an asshole because I'm nervous.

Cece: I'm sure it wasn't that bad. We'll tell him. Don't worry.

Me: I just told him, and I quote, "I want to burger with you."

Cece: Gif of rolling around laughing.

"Can we deal you in?" Jay called from across the room.

I glanced up from my phone. "Sure." I needed something to think about besides my baby mama—and her father.

After a few hours and one nothing call, I was laughing at the BS the guys were throwing out.

"Rummy," Jay said as he laid his cards on the table.

I looked up at the sound of footsteps on the stairs, coming face to face with Cece, who was wearing tight capri leggings and a yellow tank top.

Cece's smile was wide and bright. The showstopping type of smile that made it hard to want to look at anything else. A funny feeling hit me square in the chest. Because I wanted that smile to be for me only. But we weren't in that type of relationship. Before my face could give me away, I whipped my gaze back to the cards in my hands.

Hold on. What the hell was she doing here? She couldn't be here to see me. The air was pulled from my lungs. No way was she here to tell her dad about the baby, right? I had said we needed to, but she wouldn't do it *now*, would she?

No. That would be the worst possible way to tell him. In his office while he was at work? Cece wouldn't bring it up here.

I tracked her out of the corner of my eye as she headed toward the offices. Specifically, her dad's office. My heart pounded. What should I do?

Stop her. Stop her. Stop her.

"Owen?"

"Huh?" I had no clue what Jay had asked me, but the look he was giving me said I was doing a shit job with my poker face.

"You in for another round?" Jay asked, nodding to the cards he was shuffling.

"What's she doing here?" I tipped my head in the direction of Brian's office, where Cece now stood just inside the doorway. The door wasn't closed, and I could just make out the tight black pants clinging to one of her long legs.

"Cece?" Jay frowned. "She stops by. You know, to see her dad?"

Right, that was a reasonable thing. To see her dad.

"You okay?"

"Yeah. Fine." Everything was fine. But I couldn't silence my whirling thoughts.

"McKinley." The bark of the chief's voice echoed through the air before Jay had finished dealing out the next hand.

I swallowed. Fuck. Now I had to go talk to them both. On shift. Why would she do this?

"McKinley." The bellow was louder.

"Owen," Jay prompted.

"Right." I cleared my throat as I made my way to the firing squad. What did I say to my boss when the man's daughter had randomly come in and dropped a bomb like *hey, your lieutenant is my baby daddy*.

Shit.

I crossed the threshold, keeping my eyes on Brian. "Sir?"

"Since when the hell do you call me sir?" Brian scoffed. "Especially when I'm the one calling you for a favor."

"Favor?" I swallowed and finally let myself glance at Cece.

There was a small line between her eyes, and her hand twitched like she wanted to reach out to me.

Please don't. Not here.

Even if I desperately wanted her to walk over and take my hand.

This was what it meant to be stuck between a rock and a hard place. I swallowed.

"McKinley," Brian barked.

I straightened and focused on my boss.

Brian's stare flicked between us once, then settled on me. "Cece needs me to get her car from Randy."

For one split second, I relaxed. Because she wasn't here to tell her father about the baby. But then Brian's words sank in.

"Who's Randy?" I whipped my head to Cece.

She hadn't mentioned anything about another guy. Now this guy had her car? What the fuck? Maybe it wasn't fair for me to demand the answer since we weren't together, but my baby was growing inside her, and I couldn't stand the idea of another man touching her.

I fought a wince. I had no right to think it, but that didn't stop the thought from pounding through my body.

She stiffened. "Uh." She watched her dad, nibbling on her bottom lip and shifting on her feet.

Shit, I was acting too intense. I drew in a deep breath through my nose, searching for calm, but my entire body had gone on alert the moment I saw her come up the steps.

"The mechanic who's changing my oil." She glanced from me to her father.

Oh. A wave of calm washed through me. I wanted to laugh at myself. I was the one who'd told her that she needed an oil change.

"Good guy. But every time she's there, he tries to upsell her, so I pick the car up and make him upsell me." Brian chuckled.

Well, yeah. Brian was intimating as hell. Of course the guy wouldn't suggest anything unnecessary to him.

"Anyway," Brian continued. "I planned to give Cece my car and then have you drop me off at my place since we're both off at the same time this afternoon."

"Sure, sir. Absolutely." I nodded.

"What's with this sir shit?" Brian leaned forward in his chair. Hazel eyes so much like his daughter's bored into me.

But I refused to squirm under the scrutiny.

"You sure are off today." Brian shook his head, his lips turning down slightly. "I'm still surprised you scheduled the oil change on your own," he said to Cece. "She never stresses about it." He looked back to me. "Usually, I get in the car and find that it's thousands of miles past due, and she's not worried."

She wasn't worried. The *Change Oil* notification came up when I had started the car the other night. And when I looked at the sticker, I realized it was three thousand miles overdue.

A small blush rose on Cece's cheeks. "Car stuff is a pain, Dad. And it runs fine even if I don't change the oil every five thousand miles."

"I'm aware that you think that." Brian chuckled, his soft gaze on his daughter.

I swallowed at the absolute adoration this man had for his girl. Maybe Cece had good reason to be leery of telling her father. It might not go as easily as telling my parents.

"Here." Brian handed Cece his keys.

She thanked him, then stepped out of the office.

Then he turned back to me. "You sure you're okay? You seem"—he looked me up and down—"rattled today."

"Just tired. Long week on call." It wasn't a lie, but it wasn't the truth either. I was about to crawl out of my skin, and I needed to get the hell out of Brian's office. "I left the guys hanging, so I better get back to rummy."

"Yeah, or Jay will be bitching." Brian chuckled and turned back to his computer.

I left the office, shutting the door behind me.

Cece stood at the table, chatting with the guys.

I needed caffeine and a minute to chill from the trauma of thinking I was about to be shot by my boss. So I wandered to the coffee pot and poured myself a mug, trying not to stare at the woman carrying my child. But it was virtually impossible when she was across the room and yet I wasn't allowed to acknowledge our relationship.

I'd just set the mug on the counter when a small shriek ripped through the air.

I didn't hesitate at the sound. In a heartbeat, I was across the room with my arms wrapped around Cece. My heart slammed against my chest, and the only thought in my head was to protect my girl from whatever had terrified her.

"Kill it, please kill it," Cece pleaded, burying herself in my chest.

Ah. It was just a spider. I should have known that from the second my Little Miss Muffet screeched. Behind Cece, the critter was crawling along the ground. I shifted and stomped on it, twisting my boot for good measure.

"Got it. You're fine." I ran my hands along her back for a moment, then dropped my arms and took one step back. "You good?"

Cece shut her eyes and shuddered.

All I wanted to do was wrap her in a hug again, but I was suddenly aware of the attention we'd garnered. Every eye in the room was on us.

"I gotta stop being such a wimp about spiders, but I hate them." Cece sighed.

"Remember when you jumped on my lap to get away from one last year?" Jay laughed.

"It wasn't that bad." Cece's hazel eyes snapped open, and she glared at him.

"Yes, it was!"

As they went back and forth, I forced myself back to where I'd left my coffee on the counter. The need to tell her dad and the rest of the fire house about us seemed like a bigger deal, because I couldn't have her here and act like she didn't mean anything.

I sighed.

"I think *I'm staying home to relax* has been the biggest lie you've ever told," Jay whispered as he stepped up next to me. "Please tell me she's not the reason you want to be at home every night."

I really didn't want to lie to one of the few real friends I had made here. But how could I tell Jay I'd knocked up the chief's daughter?

"It's complicated."

"Yeah. The way you just vaulted across the room to her makes that clear."

"She's pregnant."

Jay stole a quick glance my way, his eyes the size of saucers. "Yours?"

"Yup." I nodded, bringing my mug to my lips.

Jay planted his hands on the counter. "Well, fuck."

"Yup." That about summed it up.

13

Pregnancy Week Ten:

Your baby mama isn't crazy.
It's perfectly normal for pregnancy
to cause mood swings and bouts of
uncontrollable crying with no
warning signs.

Owen

"Isn't this amaztastic?" Cece's best friend asked as she wandered over to the sofa.

Kelly had texted me, suggesting we all hang out and get to know each other, so here I was. But it was almost awkward. Yes, Cece was having my baby, but we weren't together. We weren't an official couple. We weren't even an unofficial one. But I was getting big-time double date vibes tonight.

"I'm so glad I thought to invite everyone." Kelly plopped herself next to her boyfriend on the plush cushion.

"Cece probably loves that you invited everyone to her house." Jack laughed.

Kelly flung her hand into the air. "Who knew furniture took so long."

"Everyone." Cece scoffed as she stepped out of the kitchen with a glass of wine in her hand.

"Oh, my wine!" Kelly made grabby hands at Cece.

The woman seemed unable to keep track of anything. Jack had picked up Kelly's sunglasses and phone after she set them down in various places when they came in. Now it seemed to be Cece who was in charge of keeping track of her.

"But seriously, do you know it takes weeks to get furniture?"

Kelly's blue eyes cut quickly from her glass to me.

"Uh...yes?" I glanced at Cece, who chuckled.

"Kelly, you are the only person I know who would do this."

I scanned the room but had no idea what she meant.

Kelly sighed. "So, like, we got new furniture because we hated ours."

Jack shook his head and lifted his beer to his lips.

"Well, *I* hated it. We ordered some really cute stuff. You know—sofa, chairs, tables, TV stand. All the good stuff. And it's *so* hot. Like totes perfect for the space. No more stuffy, boring old people shit."

Cece laughed, and Jack just rolled his eyes. I would guess Jack was about thirty-five. Maybe ten years older than the girls. So I couldn't call him old people. But Jack didn't even look mad about the label. He just squeezed Kelly's leg, encouraging her to finish the story.

"So anyway. My parents' neighbors had a fire, and they have literary nothing. So being a good Sam Sara Itan—"

"Samaritan," Cece corrected.

"Same thing." Kelly waved her hand. "Basically I gave them our stuff."

"And our furniture is still six weeks from being delivered." Jack shook his head, his left eye twitching slightly.

"Babe, don't we have fun roughing it on the floor?" Kelly wiggled her brow and Jack smirked.

"Please." Cece shook her head. "I know you're in the amazing sex all the time stage, but can you not brag to those of us who only have sex once a year?"

I turned. Was she talking about me? How did she know that? Maybe I'd told her in one of my rambling moments. Or worse, maybe that first night. It was still cloudy.

She glanced at me, and a rosy blush lit her cheeks.

I wanted to groan. The woman was gorgeous, but I would forever see that blush and remember her falling apart. Coming in waves of pleasure of my doing. My dick pressed against my jeans at the mental pictures. I swallowed.

"Was that TMI?" Cece mumbled.

Oh, she was talking about her.

I shook my head and tried not to laugh as I leaned into her. I brushed against her hair, sending the floral scent wafting over me. God, I had been dreaming about that scent.

"What are the chances that two people both don't have sex for months and months, and the one time they do, bullseye?" I murmured in her ear.

A shiver racked through her as I spoke.

"Secrets aren't nice." Kelly sighed. Before either of us could respond, she tilted her head and sniffed. "What's that smell? Oh, wait, did we set a timer?" Kelly popped up and moved across the room, with Cece behind her.

After a few seconds of silence, I picked up the remote and turned on the Metros game.

"You're a New York fan?" Jack asked.

"Yeah. Accidentally...through a buddy from college. He's friends with a couple of the guys on the team."

"Really?"

"Yeah, he—shit." I snatched the remote and switched off the game when a commercial for St. Jude came on. I glanced over my shoulder to make sure Cece wasn't looking.

Luckily, she and Kelly were focused on something on the counter. Her moods had become a bit unpredictable in the last week or so. And the other day, she'd sobbed when the same commercial had aired.

I breathed a sigh of relief, and Jack raised his brows, giving me a *what the hell?* look.

"Sorry, things make her cry so—" I scratched my head. "I can't explain it. I just try to adjust, you know."

Jack chuckled and watched Kelly. "Man, I'm living in an empty house that was fully furnished a week ago. I get it." He picked up his beer and took a sip. "And I'd hate to see Cece cry too." Placing the bottle on the coffee table, he leaned in. "I know you're worried about her dad, but"—Jack's green eyes hardened, cutting into me—"Kelly loves your girl, and what Kelly loves, I love. You seem like a good guy, but if you hurt Cece, I have no problem making you disappear." He cleared his throat. "And trust me when I say it wouldn't dent my bank account to do it."

"It's not like that."

Just as I said the words, the women across the room laughed, and my gaze shot to Cece.

"I get it. I was there too. But when you realize I'm right, remember what I said." Jack grabbed the remote and turned the game back on.

I probably should have felt intimidated by Jack, but the longer the night went on, the easier the overall vibe became. Kelly was hysterical, and Jack was her polar opposite. And although I felt awkward at first, the more time went on, the more it felt like home. And I wasn't sure what to make of that.

"I get what you're saying." I adjusted the phone on my shoulder. "But right now, I can't come up there. You need to deal with Danny."

I scanned the coffee shop as I waited in line.

"What's more important than your best friend?" Pete demanded.

Easy answer.

"Cece." I pulled my shoulders back. "I know you don't really get it, but she's my priority now. And for the foreseeable future. So adjust, because that's not changing."

"Hmm."

"Work's really so busy that you can't hang out with your best friend a little?"

"I have more going on than just work."

"Since when?" I laughed.

Pete had been obsessed with his company for the last year

and a half. He hardly looked at anything else. But the silence on the other end of the phone said a lot.

"Did you meet someone?"

Pete grunted.

My eyes widened. "Seriously?"

From there, Pete caved and told me the ridiculous story.

"You're shitting me."

"Nope. Sprayed beer all over the both of us, and now she won't even talk to me. But I can't stop thinking about her." Pete groaned.

"Great first impression, asshole." I laughed as I stepped forward. There was only one more person in front of me.

"At least I didn't get her pregnant."

"Shut up. I didn't mean to knock her up—hold on." I moved up to the counter. "Can I get a grande black coffee and venti medicine ball tea, please?"

"Sure," the barista chirped.

"I thought my daughter was the only person on earth who ordered those."

The voice ripped through me, freezing me in my tracks. No, no, no. This couldn't be happening. I glanced over my shoulder.

Shit.

I shuffled around. "Hey, Chief…"

How long had Brian been standing there? Had he heard what I was saying about Cece?

"Sir?"

I spun back to the barista who was now looking at me expectantly. She nodded to the credit card machine. Oh right. I had to pay. I juggled the phone on my shoulder while I dug in my pocket for my wallet.

Pete was still yapping in my ear. "Oh wait. Is that Cece's—"

"Gotta go. Call ya back later." I hung up, then shoved my card in the reader.

"Sorry, didn't realize you were on the phone," Brian said as I stepped aside so the chief could place is order.

He hadn't heard? Thank God.

"No worries."

"Owen!" my name was called from the pickup counter.

I grabbed the white cups and turned back to my boss.

"A coffee and a tea?" Brian nodded to the cups in my hands, one brow raised.

"The tea is great for sinus and colds." Fuck. Was it? Cece drank it to settle her stomach. Would it have made more sense to say stomachache? But then why was I drinking coffee? I was floundering here.

Brian scrutinized me. "You're sick? Aren't you on call tonight?"

Yup. I was scheduled for the overnight.

"Yes. No. I mean—" I took a breath as the chief's lips turned down. "Not sick. Feeling good."

"So...the tea?" Brian tipped his chin.

Fuck.

"Maybe a bit of a cold." I forced a cough. "I'm coming down with something. Definitely feeling sick."

Sick to the stomach, to be exact. Maybe it was my heart, because it was pounding out of my chest at that moment.

"Do you need the night off?" Brian asked.

"Off? What? No!"

"So you're not coming down with something?" my boss looked confused as hell. And who could blame him? I wasn't making sense.

But I was committed now, so I had to sell it. I feigned a sniffle and brought the paper cup of tea to my mouth. The piping-hot sugary-sweet drink caught in my throat, making me cough and fight a gag.

This was gross.

The mixture of honey and lemon with the peppermint was overpowering. How the hell did Cece stand these?

"You okay?" Brian pounded on my back.

"Yep." I held up the tea and stifled another cough. "They do a great job of clearing everything out."

"Huh. Cece uses them to settle her stomach and relax her. She'd get a kick out of you thinking they clear your sinuses." Brian laughed as he reached for his coffee on the counter. "See ya later?" He lifted his white cup in farewell.

I nodded silently. We had to tell him. Because I couldn't handle much more of this.

14

Pregnancy Week Twelve:

Other than pregnancy, what causes
lightheadedness?
Too much time around the sexy man
whose hands you want all over you.

CeCe

TOUGH CHOICES. I tapped the rook and glanced back to
Owen, whose attention was on the pasta he was stirring. If I
took his bishop, it would put him in check, but then he'd use
his king to knock out my rook. Sighing, I picked up my knight
and took the pawn that was getting too close.

"Your move." I put the plastic bin upside down over the
board to protect our chess game.

When I'd found Owen playing chess on his phone last week,
I'd begged him to take me on. And I'd discovered quickly that
he was good enough to be a challenge. Neither of us had a lot of
free time to play, but so far, we'd fit in two games. I'd won the
first, and he'd won the second, so I had every intention of
winning this one.

"The cover is a smart idea. Keeps this little cutie away from
the pieces." He scratched Flame's head.

I rolled my eyes at the ridiculous scene in front of me. This
big man holding the small cat, who was soaking up all the attention. Stupid thing never let me hold him, but the demon cat
adored Owen. One of the nurses at the hospital swore that cats
chose who they liked and who they didn't. And there wasn't
always a rhyme or reason to it. But that didn't make me feel any
less salty about it.

"Okay, buddy, gotta finish the game." Owen set Flame on
the floor, and instead of running off, the cat purred and rubbed

himself against Owen's legs. "Stop scowling at me," he said. "I can't help that your cat likes me."

I shook my head and moved back to the vegetables I was cutting for salads. "I don't get it."

He shrugged, then leaned across the island to lift the cover off our game. With a hand against his lips, he studied the board. I couldn't look away. The memory of the way his full lips dominated my mouth made my breathing accelerate. Not to mention the way his shirt pulled tight against his strong shoulders and the sight of his tapered waist and tight ass. The man was gorgeous. My stomach tightened as the ache that had been building for weeks inside my flared. My body needed a release, and damn, I wished Owen would be the one to give it to me.

But we had fallen into a friendship. We spent most of our free nights together, eating, talking, watching movies, and now, playing chess. If we both had a morning off, he would come by with tea and breakfast. And his presence was something I looked forward to every day.

He shifted, pulling me out of my trance as he pulled his phone from his pocket.

"Hey, Mom," he said as his mother appeared on the screen. I turned back to the vegetables, not wanting to be caught gawking by his mother.

"Hi." She always sounded so cheery. "Is that Cece in the background?"

"Yup. We're making dinner. Everything okay?"

"Yeah, I was just thinking about you two," she said. "Cece, you still having those dizzy spells?"

I moved closer to respond, and Owen wrapped his arm around me so we could both be seen. It was almost impossible to suppress the shiver that shot up my spine as the warmth of his forearm pressed along my back. I felt lightheaded, but not because of the vertigo that had been plaguing me.

"It's been okay, Mrs. McKinley." I smiled at the woman who looked so much like her son.

"Please, I keep telling you—it's Colleen." Owen's mother waved her hand. "So they've gotten better?"

"Somewhat. It's been about a week since the last one, so hopefully I'm done with them."

Owen's fingers barely brushed against my hip, and my breath caught. I looked at him out of the corner of my eye, but he was focused on his mother. The touch must have been an accident. But God, I wanted him to touch me *on purpose* so badly.

"Good. Maybe now that you're almost in the second trimester, you're over them."

I smiled. Owen's mom was a nurse, and I loved that it gave us something to chat about.

"Are you starting to show yet?" Colleen craned her neck like she was trying to see my belly although it wasn't on the screen.

I stepped back, and Owen's arm fell away. I lifted my tank up so Colleen could see the bump that wasn't really there.

"Not so much. But my pants are getting too tight. Those rubber band things for the buttons your girls sent are lifesavers." I dropped my shirt.

Owen had come over one day with an envelope, and in an awkward *I promise I don't think you're getting fat* conversation, he'd given me the button extenders from his sisters. The way he tripped through the explanation had been adorable.

Owen chatted for a few more minutes as we finished up dinner. And once he'd hung up, he washed his hands and pulled the chicken out of the oven.

"Your parents took everything so well." I pushed my salad around the bowl, not taking a bite.

"You mean the pregnancy?" Owen looked up from his plate.

"Yeah. I don't know...I guess I expected disappointment."

He shrugged. "I've been on my own for more than ten years now. I think as long as I'm happy, they're happy. But about that..." Owen hedged.

I raised a brow.

"How are you feeling about talking to your dad? We did say we would tell him once we knew things were good. Maybe it's time?"

The idea froze me in my seat. The idea of telling my dad made me want to jump out of my skin. Maybe it was the unknowns, because normally when my father and I talked, he asked eighty million questions that I had to be prepared to answer. And right now, I didn't have any answers about what the future would look like.

"We'll tell him soon," I assured. I'd have to eventually, right?

Owen watched me for a long moment, then nodded and turned back to his meal.

15

Pregnancy Week Thirteen:

Don't fret, Dad.
Pregnancy mood swings usually let
up during the second trimester.
But they might make another
appearance in the third!

Owen

"Cece, how many times do I have to tell you not to leave the door unlocked? I can knock when I get here." I picked up her shoes and put them in the closet and hung her lab coat on the coat rack. The woman always left a trail of clutter. For as organized as her head was, she left our space a mess.

Well, her space. I was just finding any reason I could to be here. Anything from making her dinner to finishing our chess game to dropping off food for her fridge.

"The door's unlocked so I don't have to get up." But her voice cracked. Behind her glasses, her eyes were red and puffy as she looked at me and turned back to the episode of *Jeopardy* she was watching.

"What happened?" I demanded, hustling over to her.

"Linda lost." She sniffled and wiped fresh tears from her face. "This was her fifth game. She's a nurse and single mom to twins." Another sniff. "She deserved to be there more than those two idiots."

Oh. Huh.

I pulled her into a hug, comforting her so she wouldn't cry about a woman she didn't know losing a TV game show. We were quickly running out of entertainment options. A few weeks ago, she'd read an article that said babies shouldn't be exposed to violence and bad language in utero. It seemed a little overboard, but I went with it anyway. No more cop, crime, or law shows.

We tried Disney, but she cried when Nemo got separated from his dad, and then she cried at *UP* because the old man's wife died. *Wreck it Ralph* was next, because that couldn't possibly be sad. But apparently Disney can't make movies that don't have some sort of cry factor. And when Ralph wrecked Penelope's car, thinking he was protecting her, Cece sobbed.

Sports had too many St Jude's commercials. Movies had too many sad or violent parts. It was becoming impossible.

"I'm sure she'll be okay." I rubbed her back.

"I'm sorry I'm being so silly." She tucked herself into my chest.

I fought the groan that rumbled in my chest as the soft skin of her forehead brushed against my neck. Her floral scent invaded my nose, and I wanted to bury myself in it forever. For what felt like a million times over the last few weeks, my cock jumped to life and tried to force its way out of my jeans.

I needed some space, or my control would snap, and I'd claim the woman I wanted so badly that I sometimes felt like I couldn't think straight around her.

We needed something funny—laugh out loud funny. Maybe a sitcom? I racked my brain, then snatched the remote from the coffee table.

"I have an idea." I opened the Hulu app.

"America's Funniest Home Videos?" Cece chuckled as I clicked on an episode.

We were off to a great start, but ten minutes in, as a small blond toddler teetered on the edge of a curb next to a massive mud puddle, I realized my mistake. I winced at Cece's wide-eyed panic as the little curly-haired girl wobbled and, in what felt like slow motion, tipped and fell into the mud, ruining her ruffly dress and sending a rainstorm of dirty water all over.

The audience laughed, but Cece gasped.

"Oh no, the poor little girl." And just like the two-year-old on the screen, Cece burst into tears.

"She's okay." I pointed to the TV. "Look, the family is in the audience as finalists."

"I know. I—" She wiped another errant tear off her cheek. "I'm sorry. I'm just a mess. You have to be sick of hanging out with me."

I tipped her chin up and cupped her cheek. Her hazel eyes met mine, and my heart lurched, making words that were far too honest slip out. "Cece, I'm the opposite of sick of you. I'd cut off my left arm if it meant I could stay on this sofa for a few more hours just to be around you."

Her breath caught, and her eyes widened. Her teeth sank into her plush pink lip, the action holding me captive.

"Owen." It was breathy. The exact way she'd whispered my name when my lips had been nuzzling the soft skin where her neck and shoulder met. Those moments from months ago were still burned in my mind.

I shouldn't do this. Her dad was my boss. Getting involved with her could ruin my career. The life I was building here could fall part. But the woman in front of me was already the center of the life I was building. And the rest didn't matter.

16

Pregnancy Week Thirteen:

 Emotions run high during
pregnancy but did you know that
all that extra blood pumping can
make sex better?
Unless it's just the perfect guy.

CeCe

I WAS sure this would be another fleeting moment where my hormones surged, and I would be rendered breathless by the gorgeous man sitting next to me. But then Owen dropped his mouth to mine. Full lips pressed against mine as he held my face close. Desire rushed through my system and settled deep in my core. I needed this. I needed him. The second I traced my tongue along the seam of his mouth, he groaned, yanking back, then dropping his hand to grasp my thigh. I desperately wanted him to creep his hand higher. To be where I craved his touch.

"Owen," I whimpered, my heart skipping a beat.

"This can't be *not* a big deal." His attention was set on my mouth as he rolled his own lips together. "You, me, it's not…"

"What?" Was he the one not making sense? Or did the throbbing desire racing through me leave my incapable of listening?

"I—" He shook his head. "Fuck, I want you so bad I can't even think straight. But I want to be clear." His grip on me tightened, biting into my skin for just a moment. Then he relaxed his hold and brushed his thumb across my inner thigh.

Of their own volition, my hips jerked toward him.

"I know, but you need to understand." His voice rumbled through me, deep and confident. "This time, when I feel every inch of you…" He wet his bottom lip.

My core quivered. I was dying to feel his mouth on me.

"When I taste you, when I run my tongue over you so I can memorize the taste of you, of your pleasure..."

My breath caught, and I fought a groan. His words were almost as hot as his touch.

He skated his palms over my hips, pushing back into the sofa so he hovered over me, pressing his erection into my hip. His gaze snapped to mine, cutting through me as the words left his lips.

"Then. You. Are. *Mine*." He hovered a breath away from me. I felt every hot, heavy exhale dance against my lips.

"Yours?"

"Not friends. Not fuck buddies. You're my girl. *Mine*."

The word pounded through me, and I clenched my legs together.

"I don't want casual, Cece."

"I know."

Once again, our gazes met. And understanding passed. Doing this, crossing this line once again, meant moving into new territory. He wouldn't be just my baby daddy. He'd be something to me too. Boyfriend? I didn't know if he'd want that label. But he'd be something.

"If you have any doubts, speak now," Owen whispered, watching my reaction carefully.

"None."

He smiled. "Good." Then he dropped his mouth to meet mine. Warm and wet, his tongue invaded my mouth, staking his claim.

And my body burned. I needed more.

My back arched up, pressing me against him, seeking friction. My hips rocked, and my breasts rubbed. All begging.

He reached back and yanked his shirt over his head, then tossed it across the room. Then he finally complied with my unspoken request, flicking his thumb over my nipple. The featherlight touch through the thin tank top pulsed down, settling between my thighs.

"Please, Owen, I need..." I rocked my hips again, running my hands up his flat chest. Smooth, hard, the feel of his skin was fire under my fingers. I wanted more of it. The thin material of my shorts caught the harsh denim of his jeans. I moaned.

"You need what? Tell me, and I'll give it every time."

"Touch me, please. Just touch me."

"Best words ever." He dragged his rough palm along my bare skin, sliding my tank top up my torso. Goose bumps broke out as his thumb brushed the bottom of my full breast, causing my breath to catch.

"They're bigger than I remember." Owen dropped his head and rubbed his lips back and forth across my breasts. He circled one nipple with his tongue, and then the other. Then he latched on, pulling a cry from my lips and forcing my hips to thrust against his thigh. "I know, baby. But I've been waiting weeks for this. Fantasized about this. I won't rush the moment my dream finally comes true. I want to savor it."

He teased my breast until I was panting, begging for release. His hand snaked lower, dipping into the elastic of my shorts. The second he covered my pussy, my hips thrust up into his palm.

"Cece." The groan vibrated against my ear as his fingers toyed, spreading me and sinking deep inside. "Perfect pussy. Tight. Wet. And hot as fuck."

I rocked against his hand.

"That's it. Use my hand." Circling his thumb faster over my clit, he drove me closer. Then he hooked his finger and hit the exact spot that spiked intense, blinding pleasure. It spiraled through me as he drew out every iota of my release.

When I'd returned to earth, I dropped my head back and let out a sigh. Above me, Owen stood and lifted me.

"Where?" I glanced around as he hauled me to the bedroom and kicked the door shut behind us.

"I need more room," Owen said as he laid me on the comforter and stepped back to unbutton his jeans. He pushed his boxers and jeans to the floor and stepped out of them. Then he reached for my shorts and dragged them down my legs with slow intensity.

He inspected me, starting with my face and working his way lower. When he made it past my breasts, he paused. Blinking quickly, he sucked in a breath, then pressed a kiss over the small swell of my stomach. My heart squeezed. Before I could even speak, he moved, tossing my shorts onto the floor.

The mattress dipped next to me as he settled beside me, his body radiating heat against my bare skin. He tucked a piece of hair behind my ear, then trailed his fingers down my jaw and neck, then across my breast to settle on my hip.

"As much as I've wanted this, I don't have a condom with me."

I chuckled. "Seems late to worry about birth control."

He pinched me slightly. "I'm trying to do the right thing to make sure you're good here."

Wasn't that just so very Owen? Always taking care of me. It was unlike anything I'd ever experienced before him.

He leaned in, rubbing his nose lightly and dropping kisses to my neck and over my collarbone. And although I had orgasmed a minute ago, my system flared to life again at his touch. "I got tested a few weeks ago, to make sure you didn't have anything to worry about since I fucked up the condom the last time. And everything was negative."

And he'd heard the doctor tell me I was negative at my first appointment.

"We're good, Owen. Please, I want you," I said.

The breath he let out in response rushed over my skin. With a small smile, he lifted his head and claimed my mouth again, moving his body over mine and pressing me deep into the mattress.

"I'll be careful of the baby," Owen said, bracing his weight.

"He's fine. Don't worry." I wrapped my legs around his hips, and we both hissed as his cock brushed against me. "Just take me, Owen. Make me yours."

His eyes flashed, and without another second of hesitation, he rocked hard, thrusting himself fully inside me. I closed my eyes, savoring the feeling of being linked so tightly to this man.

"It's better than I remembered," he groaned, moving his hips slowly.

I stared deep into his blue eyes, watching his passion burn. With each thrust of his hips, I was pulled deeper into the blinding pleasure he was creating. Each drive created a friction like I'd never experienced, each movement more powerful. He shifted me so his pelvis brushed against my clit with every stroke, and my eyes rolled back in my head.

He found my lips once again, owning my mouth as he claimed my pussy with each fierce thrust. Until my body pulsed and burned and I couldn't hold back anymore. I exploded around him.

At my release, his thrusts became wild and fierce as he slammed into me, groaning my name.

Collapsing next to me, he buried his face in my neck. "I'm spending the night, and we're going to do that a few more times," he huffed.

And I couldn't think of anything more perfect than that.

17

Pregnancy Week Fourteen:

Topics pregnancy books don't
cover: how to effectively hide in the
shower from your girlfriend's
father.

Owen

Long blond hair brushed against my chin, and I smiled, tightening my arm around Cece's naked body. A handful of times over the last ten days, I'd woken up next to this gorgeous woman. It was like living in a dream.

And this morning was even better. Neither of us had to work, so there was no hurry. No alarms, no stress. Hell, I didn't even know where I'd left my phone last night. Maybe on the kitchen island.

"Mmm." Cece moaned.

"Morning Beautiful." I gave her ass a squeeze. "Feel good, or is your stomach iffy today?"

Cece hadn't dealt with much morning sickness in the first trimester, but she sometimes woke up feeling less than 100 percent. If this was one of those mornings, I'd run out and get her a tea, then join her in bed again to snuggle.

She pulled up, stretching, and I couldn't help but stare at the gorgeous arch of her back. Her ivory skin was so smooth, her shoulders delicate, and the whisps of long blond hair falling out of her bun gave her that just-fucked look.

My dick had already been sitting pretty erect, but it swelled at the sight.

Cece cocked her head to the side. "Is someone knocking?" She pushed off the mattress and headed out the bedroom door. I smiled at the view of her ass the whole time.

But, shit. She wasn't going to open the door like that, right? I jumped out of bed and hustled after her to remind her that she was, in fact, naked. Not that I thought she'd forget, *but* sometimes she forgot stuff like that.

I was halfway down the hall when Cece turned toward me, wide-eyed and panicked.

"Oh no," she whispered.

"What's the matter?" I asked. Was it a spider?

Instead of answering, Cece pushed on my bare chest and shoved me into the apartment's only bathroom.

"It's my dad. I forgot he was coming over." She grabbed the robe off the door and tightened the belt around herself.

I blinked. "Why is he coming over?" I glanced down. Hanging out at Cece's in my boxers would be hard to explain in any way other than *hey, boss, my dick spent half the night inside your daughter*. I winced.

She waved me off. "Just stay in here and be quiet. I'll get rid of him."

With that, she turned and shut the door quietly behind her.

She wanted me to stay in the bathroom? I sighed and raked my hand through my hair. It was past time we talked to her father. This was ridiculous.

Muffled voices echoed in the air.

"Who the hell fixed the sink?"

I had. Two days ago. I couldn't stand the dripping anymore and had changed out the washers. I'd also put a new lightbulb in the closet, and I'd oiled the hinges on the front door so it stopped squeaking. But I couldn't jump out and say *hi, it's me. I fixed it*.

"No, I don't hear any buzzing."

Oh shit, my phone was out there somewhere. What else of mine was sitting around with it? I'd been spending more and more time over at her place.

"One sec, Dad." Her voice was getting closer, and then the

door opened a crack. She tossed something black into the air, then the room went dark again.

My phone smacked my chest. I tried to catch it, but it bounced off my fingers and teetered in the air. I went for it with my other hand, but it slipped again. My heart lurched. I might think this was ridiculous, but Cece didn't. She would cry or be pissed off if this phone hit the floor and her father came in and found me. I grabbed it just before it smashed against the tile and let out my breath. My shoulders relaxed, but then the damn thing buzzed and startled me. I fumbled it again, and once again, the thing was airborne. It could not hit the damn floor. I snatched it out of the air and finally held it firmly in my grasp. I flipped it around and checked the screen. At the list of notifications, I swiped up and navigated to my unread text messages.

Pete: Last night probably wins disaster of the week. I'm just going to say it so Danny doesn't have to start the awkward conversation.

Danny: Fuck you

Pete: How could I possibly have known that Glory was coming?

Danny: Ask the chick's name, that's how.

Pete: I don't know if that would help. Glory is pretty common. They're everywhere. Kinda like Starbucks. They pop up at every corner.

Danny: You're an asshole. Owen, tell him

Pete: He seems to be radio silent. Bet he's with Cece. Man's pussy whipped.

I rolled my eyes.

Me: Assholes, just shut up. I'm hiding out in the bathroom. Cece's dad is here. So the buzzing isn't helping me.

I flicked the phone to silent because I knew the idiots wouldn't stop.

Down the hall, Cece and her dad were still chatting. So much for getting rid of him quickly.

"Wait, Dad, what do you mean use the bathroom before you go?" Cece yelled.

"Why are you yelling? For crap's sake, you're acting weird as hell this morning. I need to use the bathroom. Last I checked, you had one, right?" Brian's voice was getting closer with each word. "So let a man use the bathroom in peace."

I scanned the dark room frantically. Brian was coming in here? Shit. I yanked open the closet door, but unless I could magically contort myself into a pretzel, I wasn't fitting. I looked from the toilet to the towel rack to the vanity to the shower. Bingo. It was the only option.

Quickly, I moved the green curtain aside and stepped in, ducking slightly so the top of my head wouldn't show above the rod just as Brian opened the door.

"What do you mean wait?"

"I just thought...well, I guess no one's in there."

"Who the fuck would be in your bathroom?"

Yeah, exactly. Who the fuck would be in her bathroom.

"Ya never know. Maybe a rat or something."

"You have *rats*?" Brian's voice went up two octaves.

"Not that I've ever seen."

"So why in the name of all things holy would you think one would be in your bathroom?" Brian asked.

I shook my head and tried not to even breathe too loud. My phone flashed, and I glanced down, swiping the notification open.

Danny: You mean you're hiding from your gf's dad like you're sixteen and sneaking in the window?

Pete: Fuck, that's funny. I almost wish he'd find you.

Me: Laugh away. I'm trapped in the shower while he uses the bathroom.

Danny: Hopefully he's not a long shitter. Your legs might cramp.

Oh no. He wouldn't.

Me: Why would he come to his daughter's house to shit???

There was no way. Right? People didn't do that.

Pete: Volcanoes don't always pick the most convenient times to blow.

Danny: I'm seriously concerned about your health if you compare shitting to a volcanic explosion.

"I don't even need toilet paper. What is wrong with you?"
"Nothing. I just want to make sure you're, okay."
"I'm perfectly fine. You're acting like a nut."

Me: He's not going to shit.

Pete: Maybe he's just going to rub one off real quick.

My gut dropped, and I almost dropped the phone again. For the love of God, that couldn't happen. Just the thought of my girlfriend's father jerking off while I hid behind the shower curtain was too much for me.

> Danny: Dude, that's whack. Who goes to
> their daughter's to choke the chicken?
>
> Pete: To choke the what?
>
> Danny: Dot the i, drill for oil, burp the worm.

Burp the fucking worm. I choked back a laugh. I hated my friends.

> Me: Shut up. Both of you.

> Pete: You know what would be really funny?
> If he was one of those guys who was
> traumatized by Psycho, and he always
> checks the shower?
>
> Danny: Oh fuck, hahaha. What would
> you say?

Yeah, I hated them. And I was done with this conversation. The door shut, and footsteps moved closer to Owen. I held my breath. What would I say if Brian pulled the curtain?

Drain looks clear? Fixed this shower from dripping too? Oh, hi, Brian. What brings you to Cece's shower?

Yeah right. I'd be screwed. Cece would cry. And it would be my fault.

So no. There was no way Brian was opening this curtain. Silently, I shuffled back, hoping to remain unnoticed. Only I bumped the tile shelf holding the shampoo and conditioner. I watched in horror as one of the bottles rocked back and forth, dangerously close to the edge. It was over if it fell...but finally it settled without falling.

A zipper went down, and a steady stream hit the bowl. I had

stood next to many men in public bathrooms in my lifetime. It wasn't a thing. But crouched in this stupid tub while my boss peed less than three feet from me felt creepy as fuck. And not something I ever wanted to do again.

Brian let out a long sigh, making me wince. *Please, God, make this stop. Make it stop.*

Finally, after what felt like hours—far longer than I thought it possible for any one person to pee—the noise stopped. The water turned on and then off, and footsteps stomped from the room.

I sank against the wall and stared at the ceiling.

Finally, the curtain was pulled back, and Cece appeared.

"We have to *fucking* tell your dad."

18
Pregnancy Week Fifteen:

 The fun pregnancy app you downloaded should be better than those comparing your baby's size to fruit. But not when it reminds you that your baby is the size of your favorite bagel—the one you can't have. How rude!

CeCe

I'D HAD one patient after another for the last few hours, and this was the first time I'd had a chance to sit down. As I dropped into a chair, the pregnancy app I'd installed on my phone flashed on my screen.

This app not only compared the baby to the size of a fruit each week, but it also compared it to other random objects. This time, my baby was the size of a pear, a bocce ball, a magic eight ball, a day gecko and a lox bagel.

God, I'd killed for a lox bagel right now.

That one was from the pregnancy taboo category. Who thought it was a good idea to remind pregnant women of all the things they couldn't have? So far it had compared the baby's size to that of a sushi roll, a bottle cap from an adult beverage, and a drop of raw honey. Now my favorite bagel. Torture.

"Oh my God."

I froze at the charge nurse's voice. How had Gina snuck up on me? When would this pregnancy brain go away?

"Are you pregnant?" She plopped down in the desk chair. She tucked her long wavy hair over her shoulder and side-eyed the phone in my hand. "Whoa, fifteen weeks! How did none of us know?" Gina's brown eyes widened. "Well. It kinda makes sense now that I think about it."

I raised one brow. Although I considered Gina a friend, I

also knew the head nurse was the hospital gossip. She joked that the nosiness came from her big Italian family.

"No coffee. No feta cheese on your salads. The massive water bottle that makes your phone yell at you. I wondered why you were dieting when you're so thin. I can't believe I didn't figure it out before now."

My cheeks heated as I stole a glance around the open emergency room. But we were alone at the nurses' station. "I'm trying to keep it quiet right now."

"Keep what quiet?" Claire asked.

Oh my God. Owen couldn't possibly be here again. I peeked up at the intake desk nurse.

"What's up?" I cringed at my overly cheerful tone.

"No, no, no. What are we not telling people?" Claire grabbed the last open chair in the nurses' station and spun it toward us. "Is this about dinner man?"

"Dinner man?" Gina asked. "Wait—is dinner man baby daddy?"

"Baby daddy?" Claire's mouth fell open.

I sank in my seat. "We're not telling people." I glared at Claire. "You're not mentioning anything about Owen bringing dinner." I pointed at Gina. "And I just said we aren't telling anyone about the baby."

Claire bounced in her seat, clapping her hands. "Baby?"

I tossed my hands up in the air. "Shh." I scanned the area. "Seriously. Secret."

"Our lips are sealed." They both did the mouth zippered shut motion.

"In the last ten seconds, you've both spilled your secrets."

The phone in my hand buzzed, startling me and sending it falling to the floor. I bent over to snatch it off the floor and heaved myself back up. Unfortunately, the movement triggered the vertigo I hadn't felt in weeks. This time, it hit me like a tidal wave. I closed my eyes and braced one hand against the desk to my right. It would pass. It always did.

"Cece, you okay?" Gina placed a hand on my back.

"Just dizzy spells from time to time." I opened one eye, testing. It was starting to subside. They didn't usually last long but could come on suddenly.

"Is that normal this early?" Claire asked.

I nodded. "The doctor said it sometimes happens." Just then, I caught the flash of a white coat out of the corner of my eye. John, the head of ER, was making his way toward us. I stood, taking my time to prevent another wave of vertigo. We chatted briefly about my last patient, then he rushed away again.

"Does John know?"

I spun to Claire. "No. I haven't had the chance to tell him. That's why it needs to stay between the three of us."

"I get that, but he's a stickler for protocol." Claire eyed the man across the room. John was by the book, but he was well respected and ran the ER smoothly. That was one of the reasons I admired him. "And with the dizzy spells—"

"I know," I assured. "I'm going to tell him. Soon." But what would he say? And what about the dizzy spells? "I haven't told anyone yet. Other than Owen and my best friend."

"You haven't told your dad yet?" Gina chimed in.

"No." I plopped down in the chair.

"Are you dizzy again?" Claire asked. "Maybe you should head out. Your shift was officially done twenty minutes ago. Can you call someone to come get you?"

I didn't want to risk having another dizzy spell, especially in front of John or, God forbid, a patient. The ER was quiet, so maybe I should head home. Worry crept in. What would happen if I got dizzy or passed out in front of a patient? And shouldn't I be done with these dizzy spells by now? Or would this last my entire pregnancy?

"Maybe call baby daddy?" Gina suggested.

"No. He's on shift."

He'd leave early if I called, but that would make my dad ask questions. I sighed. We really did need to tell him soon. But man, was I dreading it. "I can call Kelly though."

The second I closed the car door, Kelly turned to me. "You know I love you and I'd do anything for you, but I'm literally the farthest from this hospital. Owen couldn't come get you?"

"He's on shift."

My phone buzzed. Speak of the devil. Owen was checking in. I responded, letting him know Kelly was driving me home and asked if he could drop me off for my shift tomorrow.

"Your dad couldn't come?" Kelly flicked her blinker and pulled onto the long, dark road that led home.

"He still doesn't know." My phone buzzed two more times, but I didn't look at it.

"Why? What are you going to do? Pretend you got fat and adopted a random newborn? Your dad is oblivious sometimes, but he's still going to wonder about the sudden appearance of a needy little person who cries all the time."

I winced.

"You gonna tell him Santa brought you a small human? Or the Easter Bunny? The Tooth Fairy? No wait, what are the big birds that barf out babies?"

"What?" Normally I could follow Kelly's thoughts, but the bird puking babies? I had nothing.

"Pelicans?" Kelly tapped her nails on the wheel. "You know those big birds that come and barf out the babies. The ones people tell their kids about?" Kelly turned and nodded, wearing a big smile.

"Kel, no one ever tells children about birds that barf babies."

"I swear I've heard that story. Maybe my parents are just weird." Kelly rolled her eyes and shrugged. "Do you have a better plan?"

"Owen and I are going to tell him." I pressed my teeth into my lower lip and glanced out the window. My phone buzzed again. "We just haven't had a chance."

Kelly glanced at her own phone. "A weird number is texting me. Why does it look familiar?" Dismissing the notification, she continued on. "Didn't your dad come over the other morning?"

"Ugh, that was a disaster." I tried not to laugh at the memory.

"What happened?"

"We were in bed when he showed up, and Owen ended up hiding behind the shower curtain while Dad peed." I chuckled.

Kelly snorted, her head jerking between me and the road. "You cannot be for reals right now."

"Oh, but I am."

"I don't know what you're waiting for—"

My phone rang. "Owen's calling."

The second I answered, Owen barked in my ear. "What's the matter? Why is Kelly driving you home? Are you okay?" he asked, rapid-fire. "Why aren't you answering my texts? Kelly didn't even answer me. Why didn't you call me?"

"Owen, take a breath. I'm fine. Just got a little dizzy and didn't think I should drive home. You're at work anyway."

"I get off in a half hour. I could have left a little early."

"Yeah, but Dad would have wondered why."

He scoffed out a breath and snapped, "Right. But I'm coming over to check on you when I get off."

"Fine. Yes." I hung up, feeling guilty. For not having told my dad yet. For worrying Owen. For making Kelly drive all the way out of her way. I hated feeling so out of control. I flopped my head back against the leather headrest and watched the scenery out the front window.

"The stork!" Kelly shouted. "That's the one that barfs babies."

I sighed. "Yeah, Kel—the stork brings babies."

"Want me to just be quiet?"

"Yes," I said, closing my eyes and sinking farther into my seat. People always talked about pregnancy being exhausting, but I'd really had no idea.

"Do you want me to walk you in?" Kelly asked as she pulled into a parking spot at my complex fifteen minutes later.

"No. I'm fine." Truthfully, I could have driven myself home.

"You sure? Flame won't get out, right?"

That would be the cherry on top of this crappy afternoon. "That demon better not leave the house."

Kelly chuckled. "Okay. Love you. Call me if you need anything."

After a warm shower, I tossed dinner into the oven. I was just settling on the couch when the front door opened.

Owen closed the door and tossed the shoes into the closet, then made his way farther into the apartment. He slung the strap of his duffel off his shoulder and let it fall to the ground at his feet. Blowing out a breath, he crossed his arms over his chest like he was bracing for a fight. "My stuff," he said as he nodded to his bag. "I'm staying with you."

I hadn't meant to make him so worried that he'd upend his life to take care of me. "Owen, I don't want to disrupt your routine or force you to be here with me."

"This is for my own peace of mind. I'm a hell of a lot more disrupted when I don't know that you're okay."

If staying with me would give him a peace of mind, then how could I tell him no? Especially since I was the one who'd made him unnecessarily worried in the first place.

"If you're sure..."

"I've never been more sure of anything."

19

Pregnancy Week Sixteen:

 About this time people start thinking
about the nursery...normally the
question is what color?
Not are we having one or two?

Owen

I LIVED for mornings like this. When neither of us had to rush out of bed, and she could stay curled up in my arms. The curve of her body fit so perfectly against mine. I ran my hand down her flat stomach and stopped at the small bump.

Was that...? I smiled. *Our baby* was growing inside her.

Cece rolled toward me, lying flat on her back as I propped myself up on an elbow, keeping my hand nestled over her lower belly.

"Can you feel our little guy?"

"I think so—kinda feels like butterflies." Her hazel eyes shimmered with joy. "But you probably won't be able to feel him for another month or so."

I couldn't wait for that moment. Feeling my baby move under her soft skin would be one of those moments to live for.

"I wish I was off today." I wanted to stay here. In this moment. But my shift started at noon, and I still needed to stop by my apartment.

"You could have skipped the extra shift," she teased.

Maybe. But as ready as I was to tell her dad, I had to be prepared for Brian's anger. And that could be the end of my job at the fire house.

So not only did I need to stockpile all the hours I could now, but I needed to consider what I'd do if I couldn't be a firefighter. I hated the idea, but Cece and our baby were worth it.

So I'd been picking up more EMT shifts and planned to start paramedic training. I wanted to look into the class schedule that would work the best for Cece and the little guy.

"I want to work now so I can be around more when the little man is here. So I really need to get up," I said as I swung my legs over the side of the bed. Instantly, I missed the warmth of her body. "Need to grab some stuff before my shift."

"Owen—"

I turned toward her, sensing the hesitation in her voice.

"I haven't had any dizziness all week." She sat up, holding the sheet against her chest. "You don't have to keep staying here."

Was she serious? Knowing she and the little guy were safely tucked in my arms gave me a peace that I didn't have at home—my quiet, empty apartment. When I went home, there was no clutter to clean up, no cat rubbing against my leg, no beautiful blonde smiling at me.

"Do you not want me here?" It was hard to meet her eyes as I asked the question. Because if the answer was no, it would crush me. If the answer was no, then our visions of the future were very different.

She shook her head, making my heart stop. "That's not what I meant. I do want you here."

The breath whooshed out of my lungs, and I sagged in relief.

"But," she continued, "I know how important home is to you. If you want to be at your place again, I get it."

"Home *is* important to me." I tucked a long piece of hair behind her ear and scooted closer. "But home isn't my apartment anymore. It's wherever you and little man are."

She blinked rapidly, fighting tears, but a slight smile lifted her lips. "Okay."

I wrapped my arm around her back.

"But…"

She stiffened, pressing her teeth into her bottom lip.

I hated the nervous look on her face, but we needed to be on the same page about this. "We need to talk about what we're doing once the baby comes."

"What do you mean?" She swallowed.

"I mean—are we getting two cribs? Two highchairs? A parenting schedule? You know..."

She blinked back tears again, but this time, her lips formed a tight line.

Shit. Like an asshole, I was making her upset. But I had to ask, even though the look in her eyes made my heart squeeze. "Like two separate homes?"

"Is that—" She swallowed harshly. "What you want?"

"No." But I wouldn't force her into it. "But if that's what you want—"

She shook her head violently. "That's *not* what I want either."

I let out a long breath and smiled. "So, Cece Thompson, do you want to officially move in together?"

"Yeah." She nodded, and a few tears slipped down her cheek. I wiped them away and gave her a quick kiss.

"You have the two bedrooms, so it makes sense to be here for now, don't you think?" I asked.

"Hopefully management will let us work out something with the leases."

"Tomorrow problems," I assured. Right now, we had something more pressing to deal with. "And we need to tell your dad."

"Of course. We will. Soon."

I nodded. Though I couldn't help but feel like that response was a brush-off.

20

Pregnancy Week Seventeen:

 Normally people panic
when labor starts.
Not in the second
trimester...

CeCe

I TOOK a sip of my cold water. I smirked as Savannah Williams gave her brother Rhett a hard time. The Williams family owned The Dock, the local restaurant and marina, and I had gone to school with Savannah. When Savannah and Kelly got together? Look out world.

"Sorry I'm late, chickadee." My father dropped into the chair across from her, stealing my attention from the Williams siblings.

"I'm used to it. I swear I've spent more of my life waiting on you," I joked, setting my glass on the table and leaning over to give him a quick peck on the cheek.

"This time it wasn't my fault. I'm drowning in paperwork." He shook his head. "I think it's time to put Owen on a daytime schedule so he can take over some of the office stuff. But he's been maxing out his time with his regular duties and EMT shifts, so I'm not sure he's interested in office work."

That was the opposite of true. Owen would jump at the chance for a promotion and a set schedule. Some people might not like the politics and paperwork that came with the higher ranks, but Owen wanted to move up.

"Have you talked to him?"

My dad shook his head and shrugged. "He's been acting weird lately, but I'll pull him in this week and sort it out."

"You finally made it, old man? I thought you were standing

your daughter up," the blond Williams sister joked as she stood at our table.

"Savannah." my father shook his head with a chuckle. "Good to see you."

"As much as I love seeing Cece, I prefer when you bring your fire boys, Chief Thompson. The man candy at your firehouse is per-fect-ion." Savannah did a little shake.

"Just get us the usual, Savannah."

"The usual. Got it." She winked and turned to leave.

"Uh, wait," I called. "No feta on mine, please."

Savannah's blue eyes narrowed, and she smirked. "No feta, huh?" Her gaze shot between my father and me. "Got it."

I sighed. I probably should have just picked off the cheese. Because now the gossip would start. It was a good thing I had met my dad here tonight to make plans to have him over for dinner with Owen. Now that we'd talked about where things were going and what life would be like when the baby came, I was more than ready to share the news with my father.

"Diet coke with lime, because lemons are for losers." Savanah placed the drink in front of Cece's father. "More *water*, Cece?" Savannah raised my brow.

"I'm fine, thanks."

Savannah smirked and trotted away.

"So, Dad." I swallowed. "I've been seeing someone."

His brows shot up, and he poked his tongue into his cheek and grunted as he digested the news. "How long?"

"A few months."

He nodded. "Makes sense. The sink got fixed. And the oil change. Hell, I think the guy changed your wiper blades and fixed that damn squeak in your front door too."

That was my dad's version of *I don't hate the guy yet.*

"He is handy."

"Point in his favor." He picked up his drink and took a sip.

"So I guess this lunch is a *hey, dad, get ready to meet the guy who's taking your place as most important male in my life.*"

"Dad." I chuckled and rolled my eyes at his drama.

"I'm teasing," he assured. "But I would like to meet the guy." He shrugged. "It's my responsibility to scare the shit out of him and all."

"I was thinking—"

"Bacon burger, double patty for Dad." Savannah set the burger down. "And Greek salad, no feta, for Cece."

"Thanks," my father said.

I waited for Savannah to leave before I started again. "I was thinking sometime this week..." I reached for my napkin roll and unwound my silverware. "Maybe Thursday, since it works for my schedule—" The fork slipped out of the napkin and fell. It bounced off my lap, then dropped to the floor. "Shoot." I bent quickly and scooped it off the floor.

The second I sat back up, I realized my mistake. I'd moved too fast. The wave of vertigo hit, and my vision swam. I blinked, hoping to fight through it, but the dark spots took over, and everything went black.

21

Pregnancy Week Seventeen:

People always joke that kids give their moms heart attacks, but no one warns dads-to-be that it happens to them too.

Owen

I GLANCED up from my phone as the radio crackled. It had been quiet for the last four hours. I'd gotten halfway through *We're Pregnant: The Dad-to-Be Guide.* Instead of general chatter on the radio, the tones for the bus sounded loudly.

"Bus twenty-one, respond to an unresponsive twentysome-thing female at The Dock, Three Marine Drive. Repeating..."

It was barely past noon, so it was a bit early for drunk college girls. Normally, the night shift dealt with the puking route.

"She'll probably love it when your face is the first thing she sees when she comes to," Terri teased.

I snorted. The woman got a kick out of how drunk girls reacted to me. I used to find it funny, but lately, it was just a nuisance.

Setting my phone down, I stood and stretched as the radio crackled again.

"Sensitivity warning for all..." I tipped my head and waited for the information. "The patient is Chief Thompson's daughter."

I froze, and ice ran through my veins as I listened to dispatch repeat the information. Not Cece. My breath sped up as my heart pounded in my ears. I didn't realize I was moving until I was standing in front of the ambulance with Terri yanking on my arm.

"*Owen*." How many times had she said my name?

Wide-eyed, I glanced over to her. With one hand on my arm, she gestured for me to stop with the other. But I couldn't.

"Slow down. Deep breath."

I didn't have time to breathe. We needed to get to The Dock. I brushed her off and hustled to the driver's side.

"I'll drive," Terri assured. I opened my mouth to argue, but she cut me off. "You're not in the right headspace. I'll get us there fast and safe."

Not wanting to waste time arguing, I simply rushed around the front of the white and red ambulance and climbed in.

"I'm not a gossip," Terri said as we pulled out onto the road with our lights and sirens flashing, "but I'm not stupid either. You bring the chief's daughter lunch and dinner every time we work together. And the way you smile when you see her tells me you're a bit too personally involved to handle this call rationally. So if you need me to take lead..."

I turned to Terri, who hadn't once commented about Cece in all the shifts we'd ridden together. I hadn't thought she noticed, but as it turned out, she just respected my privacy.

I swallowed. I prided myself on my level head in any situation. I fisted my hands to stop the trembling. "I'll be fine."

"Then you head in when we get there, and I'll get the stretcher." Terri didn't look thrilled, but she also didn't put up a fight.

Before the ambulance had fully stopped, I hopped out and grabbed the go bag, then took off at a run to the front entrance of the restaurant. I scanned my surroundings as I moved, finding Cece sitting on the floor, leaning against a chair at a small table. Her father kneeled next to her, as did the young owner of the place. Cece glanced my way, and our eyes met. Just seeing her alert lightened the feel of the ball of lead that had taken up residence in my stomach the moment I'd heard it was her.

"McKinley," Brian barked.

My attention snapped to my boss.

"Thank God you're here." The Chief stood and stepped back, making room for me. "She was talking to me one minute, and then she was out cold on the floor the next. She completely fell out of her chair."

"Dad, I'm fine. I told you—it was just low blood pressure. You could have taken me to the hospital. The ambulance is overkill."

She was tucked in on herself. The position seemed odd, until I realized she was cradling her stomach.

"Give me some room, sir," I said to the dark-haired man on Cece's other side. When he'd complied and pushed to his feet, I bent down and reached for Cece's arm.

Her skin was cold to the touch as I slid my fingers to her wrist to find the pulse. My hands quivered, and Cece once again met my eyes.

"I think I landed on my shoulder. Not my head or... anything." The arm around her stomach tightened, and her eyes swam with fear, even as she assured me.

I wanted to hug her and make her feel better. Hell, it would make me feel better. I wanted to assure us both that Cece and our little guy were fine. But I had to put all my emotions in a box and do my damn job.

"Does it hurt?" I checked her shoulder, neck, and head. All seemed fine. Terri came up behind me with the stretcher as I was checking her blood pressure.

"Sixty-seven over eighty-eight. Her O2 is 98 percent. Pulse seventy-four." I rattled off her vitals as I tugged at the Velcro of the pressure cuff wrapped around my girlfriend's arm and stood up. "Seems like a low-pressure issue."

Terri helped me get Cece onto the stretcher and strapped on. I moved to the head of the stretcher, ready to get her loaded, hoping for a moment alone in the ambulance so we could talk.

"I'm coming," Brian demanded as we rolled her toward the door.

"What? No, Dad. Just take your car." Cece sighed.

"No. If being the fire chief gets me one perk, it's that when my only child is being transported by ambulance, I get to ride along." He crossed his arms over his broad chest like he was prepared for a fight. But after the last fifteen minutes, I understood all too well what it was to worry about a loved one.

"Sure thing, Chief." I ignored the glare Cece sent me, along with my own desire to have her alone. Because this was my job. Even if it sucked.

With Brian's eyes on his daughter, I could be nothing but professional. Five minutes out, I filled out the Twiage app, noting that she was seventeen weeks pregnant. I understood what putting that information into the system meant, and the guilt joined the worry that I was doing my best to lock away.

We pulled up, and Brian helped me get the stretcher out of the back. I went through the motions, keeping my emotions buried deep. Claire sat at the desk, watching all of us with wide eyes.

"You okay, Cece?" she asked.

"This is overkill."

I almost snapped at the statement. It most certainly wasn't overkill. She was pregnant and had passed out. Both she and our baby needed to be checked. And I was pretty sure she knew it.

"Why don't we get Dad into the waiting room while Owen gets Cece set up in room three?" Claire directed Brian, despite his argument about staying with his daughter.

"I'll give you two a minute," Terri said once we got Cece onto the bed.

I studied Cece where she sat on the white sheet that covered the emergency room bed. I lifted the railing on the side just in case she got dizzy again. Although I should be here as Cece's boyfriend and the father of our child, I wasn't. The idea of leaving this room burned my gut, but the longer I stayed, the harder it was to keep myself in check. I leaned down, and with the floral scent of her perfume overtaking my senses, I kissed the top of her head.

"Let me know what they say."

She nodded silently, keeping her eyes downcast.

With that, I turned and headed out of the room. I had no reason to pause at the desk. No reason to ask questions. My job was done. And yet I desperately wanted an excuse to stay.

"Owen."

I turned at the sound of Jay's voice. "What are you doing here?" I asked.

"Heard the tones." Jay placed a hand on my shoulder. "I know you can't stay, man. I figured I could hang out and keep you updated."

I closed my eyes and swallowed past the lump in my throat. It had only been a few months, but Jay had become a better friend than I deserved. "Thanks."

"What are friends for?" Jay dropped his hand and headed into the waiting room with the chief.

22

Pregnancy Week Seventeen:

There's lots of advice for telling your boss you're preggo out there, but none of it says how to do it from a hospital bed while he's reading your chart.

CeCe

"I HEAR CONGRATULATIONS ARE IN ORDER." My boss John stood at the door, chart in hand.

I winced. This was why I didn't want to be rushed here by ambulance. Now the entire hospital knew I was pregnant.

"I—We..."

But John held his hand up and snapped the metal chart closed.

"By law, you're not required to notify your employer of your pregnancy." John set the chart on the rolling tray. "Let's check everything out, and then we can talk."

He rolled in a portable ultrasound machine, and once he confirmed baby was happy and unharmed by the day's events, he dropped into the chair next to me.

"We'll run blood work, but I assume the blood pressure drop was the reason you passed out. I see in your notes that this has been an ongoing issue."

I swallowed. Although I was relieved that the baby was doing well, the stress of the day was creeping up.

"I promise it hasn't affected my work."

John sighed. "Cece, you're a consummate professional. I have no doubt that if you were concerned about patient safety, you would have had someone else take over. And truthfully, you're not a surgeon or part of the emergency response team, so if you need to sit or slow down for a minute, it won't hurt our patients. We can help make this easier on you."

"Okay." I took in a deep breath and let it out.

"But," he continued, "there is a note in here that your father isn't aware. And since there isn't another person here with you, I want to make sure you have support outside the hospital."

"I do." I cut him off. "My boyfriend lives with me, and he's wonderful."

John fought a smirk. "Does he happen to be the EMT who goes out of his way to see you every time he's in the building?"

"Uh." I blinked.

John laughed. "I'm not looking to get anyone in trouble. But secrets tend to cause stress. And I don't think you need any more of that right now. So my advice would be to try to limit it, and maybe let the people who care about you know what's going on so they can help."

I nodded.

"Okay. I'm giving you the next three days off to rest."

"I don't—"

"I'm serious. If I wasn't your boss, I'd be writing a note for your employer. We'll see you Friday. Enjoy the time. And maybe talk to your dad." John stood. "I'll get you discharged."

Twenty minutes later, I was wheeled out to Jay's waiting car.

"You'll follow up with them this week, right?" My father asked from between the front seats.

"Yes, but like they said, it's just low blood pressure. I'm fine." I shut my eyes.

I'd texted Owen a few times, but he'd only sent one-word responses. It was hard to know if he was busy or mad. Or something else. Waiting to tell my father really had turned into more than it needed to be. I wanted it all out there at this point. But I'd have to wait a little longer, because Owen deserved to be part of the conversation.

I peeked at Jay, who hadn't looked happy since the moment I stepped into the waiting room. I didn't know why he was there, but I was grateful my father hadn't waited alone.

We pulled into The Dock parking lot, and Jay turned to my father. "I'll drop her by her place, boss. You two can deal with the car tomorrow."

My father narrowed his eyes on Jay, then turned that expression on me. "Is that what you want?"

I nodded.

He squeezed my shoulder. "Call me tonight, okay?"

"Yes. Love you." I watched him get in his car as Jay pulled out.

"I realize I've known you forever, but I'm team Owen. You're not being fair to him, Cece." Jay frowned.

"He told you." I swallowed.

Jay gave a clipped nod. "A few weeks ago. He's a good friend and a stand-up guy. Not to mention one of the best lieutenants we've ever had. He deserved to be with you today. You need to fix this shit."

I stared out the window. "I know."

23

Pregnancy Week Seventeen:

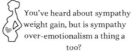 You've heard about sympathy weight gain, but is sympathy over-emotionalism a thing a too?

Owen

SHOWERED AND CHANGED, I paced across the wood floor next to the island in our kitchen. Jay and Cece had both texted that they were on their way. I gave them both an okay, but that was the most I could handle without exploding.

I switched between pissed off and frustrated as hell. Terri had called my relief to come in three hours early, but coming home hadn't helped my mood. Because I'd been stuck here, waiting for texts updates from Jay or Cece.

And although I was beyond thrilled that the baby and Cece were fine, Cece and I needed to have a serious talk. There was no way I could live through something like that again. I'd been beyond patient about her putting off telling her father, but now I was done with that shit.

If the chief wanted to fire me, then fine. I'd figure it out. But I wouldn't sit on the sidelines when my family had an emergency again. I slammed both palms on the counter and turned one way, then the other, cracking my back. Worst day of my life. I was working on calming breaths when the lock turned. And then there she was. My girl stood in the doorway, looking tired and sad and just done.

Our eyes met for one beat before we moved toward one another. I met her halfway through the living room and wrapped her tight in my arms. All the tension in my body disappeared at the feel of her, and a thick lump formed in my throat.

Ten seconds ago, my body had been coursing with frustration and anger. But now I was so swamped with relief that I was getting choked up.

I lifted her into my arms and sat on the sofa, tucking her against me, enjoying the tickle of her hair on my neck. This was where she belonged.

"Owen—"

"Shh," I croaked. "I need one minute to hold the most important things in my life, and then we can hash shit out. After today, you're giving me that. Even if I have to pretend I see a spider to scare you into staying in my arms."

And I wasn't above playing the bug card to keep Little Miss Muffet exactly where she was.

"No spiders needed. I'm happy to stay in your arms forever." The content sigh left her lips and melted into me.

I gave us a minute just to be before I jumped right into the deep end.

"I don't know why you don't want to tell your dad, babe, but no matter how he reacts, we've got this." I tightened my arms around her.

"Owen—"

But I wasn't done. "If he fires me. I'll get my paramedic certification and work for the hospital. If he hates me because I'm not good enough, I promise I'll do everything in my power to show him I'm worthy of you."

"Owen—"

"I mean it. Even if I have to sit on his front porch every day to get him to talk to me. Whatever you need, I've got you. I love you, Cece."

She pulled back and stared up at me. "You love me?"

I gathered her close again. "So fucking much I can't stand it."

"I love you too."

The words ripped through me, sending me on a high I didn't think was possible after the long, awful afternoon.

"Best words ever." I pressed my lips lightly against her head. "Regardless of why you don't want to tell your dad, I promise you—we can handle it."

She chuckled.

"What?"

"I was at The Dock with my dad today so I could tell him I'm dating someone. I asked him if he could come over on Thursday to meet my boyfriend."

"Oh." I smiled. "Good. It's about damn time."

All I could do now was hope that the Chief took the news well.

24

Pregnancy Week Eighteen:

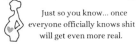 Just so you know... once everyone officially knows shit will get even more real.

CeCe

ALTHOUGH HE'D BEEN the one who was eager to break the news to my dad, he was a ball of nerves now that the moment had arrived. It was almost comical watching him pace the kitchen as Flame mimicked his movement on the island.

I had to chuckle at all the restless energy. Shockingly, I wasn't feeling any at all. The news would surprise my dad, sure, but I had a plan. And in the end, I knew he'd adore his grandchild.

Owen finally stopped pacing and turned back to the alfredo sauce simmering on the stove.

"We got this," I said, sidling up behind him and wrapping my arms around his waist.

He sagged into me. "I know."

The knock echoed around the open concept space, and Owen tensed again. "Relax."

I popped up on my toes and pressed a kiss to his lips. He sighed into my mouth. "Please don't make me do the official meet your dad thing with a boner, Cece."

With a laugh, I headed for the door. Standing on the other side, my father was dressed in jeans and his typical Half Moon Lake FD polo. I smirked when I realized he and Owen were matching. Hopefully, he'd find it funny too. Even if things got off to a rough start, I knew the two most important men in my life would eventually get along perfectly.

"Hey, Dad."

He placed a kiss on my cheek and handed me a bottle of white wine. "So where's this g—" Two steps into my apartment, his eyes widened, and he froze. "McKinley?"

"Sir." Owen swallowed thickly, watching my father with a wary expression.

My dad cocked his head and chuckled. "I figured it was Jay, but this makes a hell of a lot more sense. After all that sir shit, I should have realized." He strode over to Owen and slapped him on the back. "And this means when I come over for dinner, the food will be edible. I wasn't sure whether to be more worried that Cece was cooking, or Jay."

"Dad!" I scoffed. "I can cook."

He smiled. "But not as well as your boyfriend. I love Jay, but I gotta tell you, I'm glad it's not him."

"Why did you think I was dating Jay?" I shook my head.

"What kind of man comes to sit with his boss for three hours at the hospital?" He shook his head and laughed.

"A good friend who knew I was riding and freaking out." Owen sighed.

"Very true." My dad tilted his head and took a deep breath. "Smells great."

"It'll be ready in a few minutes. Do you mind if we sit and talk first, sir?"

"*That* sounds ominous." My father glanced at me. "Is something wrong?"

I went to the fridge and pulled out a beer for my dad, then passed it across the island to where he'd dropped into the stool. Owen tucked his arm around my waist.

My dad homed in on the contact, but Owen didn't pull back. In fact, he tightened his grip.

"Going to take some getting used to, I guess." With a shake of his head, my dad took a sip of his beer.

Owen looked down at me. We had decided I would break the news.

"We'd love if you got used to it, because Owen and I are moving in together, and I'm pregnant." Might as well just get everything out in the open.

My father sputtered and coughed. "I'm sorry. *What*?" He shot to his feet.

Owen shook his head and rolled his eyes at me, then rounded the island. "Chief," he said, looking him in the eye, "you raised an amazing woman. I'm beyond lucky to even know her. It's all happened fast, but I love your daughter, and for some crazy reason, she feels the same way." Owen sent me a small smile. "So although it's not happening on the timeline you might have liked or in the traditional order, I promise to spend the rest of my life being everything you could want for her to have in a partner."

Owen held his hand out.

My dad looked at Owen's hand, then turned to me. Finally, he sighed.

"You make it really hard not to like ya, Mc—Owen." My father took the offered hand, then turned back to me, his eyes going soft. "So when are you...due? Summer baby?"

"March," I corrected.

He whipped around and glared at Owen.

"We met before I knew she was your daughter." Owen's words were careful. Like he was trying to lessen the blow of *I slept with your daughter the first few weeks I was in town*.

My dad grunted. "Been keeping this secret for a while."

"Yeah." I moved around the counter to take my boyfriend's hand. "You're a man who wants answers to all the questions. And I'm sure you can see how, at first, Owen and I wouldn't have had the answers. We needed some time to figure out how this would go."

My father gave a clipped nod. "So the fainting spell was pregnancy related? All is well?"

I nodded. "Yes, the baby and I are fine, but it did show me how much this conversation needed to happen. Because it hit us both hard. Not being together during something like that was painful, and we don't want that anymore."

Owen squeezed my hand twice. "When she needs me, I'll be there."

My father banged his hand flat on the counter. "It's not ideal, but honestly, you've been an asset to me so far. Everything I know says you're a good man, so I guess that means my daughter's lucky to have you."

Owen's relief at those words was like a force in the room. His entire body lightened, like a weight was lifted from his shoulders.

"But," my father added, picking up his beer bottle and pointing it at him, "you've been burning the candle at both ends, working max hours every week. You have a family that needs you now, so my advice, not that you have to take it, is to back off the EMT shit and come work more hours with me. We'll do the bureaucratic bullshit together, and we'll work out more of a set schedule before the baby comes. We'll work on teaching you to do my job someday."

Owen shut his eyes, even as the smile hit his lips. He swallowed and nodded. "That used to be the dream."

I spun so I was facing him. "You don't want that?"

He chuckled. "I do, babe. But now the dream is you and the little guy. The rest is just extra." His gaze cut back to my father. "But I'd love that, sir."

My dad nodded and focused on me. "For the record, I understand waiting to tell me until you got your ducks out of the muck and in a row. But I love you, Cece, and I will support you always. And your child or children. And"—his eyes cut to

Owen again—"your partner. Who better eventually have a title more like spouse."

Owen laughed but nodded. "Heard."

"So no more secrets, yeah?"

I let go of Owen's hand and hugged my dad tight. "I love you, Dad."

25

Pregnancy Week Nineteen:

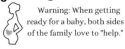 Warning: When getting ready for a baby, both sides of the family love to "help."

Owen

I DROPPED the box of kitchen stuff on the island. Today, it would be official. Cece and I would be living together. Since we were emptying my apartment, my parents and sisters were coming from Richmond to help. My family meant well, but they were like wrecking balls. Not always a bad thing, but definitely always a lot.

"Remember what I told you about my sisters," I said as Cece began unpacking the box.

"It'll be fine."

"They will try to come in and take over." I handed her a coffee mug from the box. "Just be strong and don't let them talk you into anything you don't want to do."

Cece shook her head. "You worry too much." She turned, placing the mug in the cabinet. "Besides, I lived with Kelly for years, and I never let her get rid of *our* furniture, so I think I can handle your sisters."

"Famous last words."

A knock on the door had me taking a deep breath before making my way to let my crazy family in. After my mom and sisters greeted me with hugs, they immediately swarmed Cece, chatting with her like they had known her for years.

"Took you long enough to invite us down. Your mother has been chomping at the bit since you told her Cece was pregnant." My dad eyed the group of women.

157

"I know." I helped my father carry in a few bags of things, wincing as I noticed plants in one of them. My sisters. I'd told them plants were a no-go because of Flame. "How was the drive?"

"They spent the entire time yapping. I think your sisters are just excited to have a weekend away from the kids." My father chuckled. "I feel bad for Joe and Kevin."

I didn't. I knew how much my sisters did for their families on a daily basis, and they deserved time away like this.

"So, you ready for all this?" My father nodded at Cece.

"I don't know..." I wasn't sure if my father meant moving in with Cece or becoming a dad. But my answer was the same regardless. "I'm afraid of messing it up."

"Eh, that'll always be the case. Most days, I still feel like that."

Leave it to my dad not to beat around the bush.

"Just love them both and remember to put them first, and you'll be fine, Owen." He glanced to the women again. "So is it just the two of us moving the furniture?"

"No. I have help coming."

There was another knock on the door a few minutes later, and then Brian and Jay joined the group in the living room as Cece started going over the plan for the day.

"We went through Owen's apartment and tagged all of his stuff."

I chuckled. *Cece* went through my place. I told her it didn't matter to me, and she was free to decide what we wanted to keep, store, and get rid of.

She sent me a look with one eyebrow cocked before continuing. "Green Post-its mean storage, pink for our place, and blue for giving away."

"We'll start with taking the stuff to the storage—"

"By that, you mean my basement, right?" Brian interjected.

"Yes." I awkwardly laughed. "I appreciate you letting me store most of my stuff in your basement."

"Cece doesn't love your bachelor pad furniture?" Jay teased.

"What?" Cece widened her eyes, looking between me and Jay. "No, his furniture is great. But—" she stuttered. "It just didn't make sense to have to move my stuff out and his stuff in. Moving stuff once made the most sense. Right?" She looked at me, eyes pleading.

"Yeah, babe." I walked over to her and wrapped my arm around her shoulders before placing a kiss to her temple. I glared at Jay over her head. Hoping the message was clear.

"Oh yeah, that totally makes sense." Luckily, I wouldn't have to punch one of my best friends for making my girl cry.

After the guys and I brought in the boxes of stuff that were in my car for the women to unpack, we loaded up the furniture from my place and dropped it off in Brian's basement.

"Why don't we pick up lunch for everyone from The Dock?" Brian suggested as we left his house.

"Yeah." I pulled out my phone. "I'll call Cece and see what the girls want."

An hour later, I walked in with the food and placed the bags on the kitchen island. Jay handed out beers to the men, and I headed to the back of the apartment where I heard the women's voices. I stepped into the extra bedroom that would be the nursery and froze, taking in Cece, my mom, and my sisters, all with paint brushes in hand.

"What are you doing?" I asked. "I thought we were waiting to paint the nursery."

One wall was almost completely navy blue. Cece put her brush down and came over to me. "Your sisters are super resourceful." She shook her head. "One minute, we were talking about how I was thinking a navy blue would be perfect for the nursery, and then half an hour later, they had paint and brushes. I don't know how they managed it."

159

"Mom made you sit and drink some water while I ran to hardware store." Maggie didn't even look away from the wall.

Cece just shrugged. I'd warned her. It was just how my sisters were.

"I told you. Remember the plants and towels?"

"I like it though." She shrugged. "It'll look so good with the sailboats."

"Probably but, I keep telling you it's a girl. Wasn't wrong about you, I'm not wrong about this princess either." Brian stepped into the doorway to the room. "You guys are so screwed." He shook his head before turning and heading back out with a chuckle.

But no way Cece and I could both be wrong.

26

Pregnancy Week Twenty:

People always tell you kids constantly surprise you, but you won't get it until you have one of your own.

CeCe

I SHIFTED, the paper gown crinkling as I moved.

"You okay?" Owen placed his warm hand on my knee. "Comfortable?"

I side-eyed him. Did he really think sitting on paper while swathed in a paper gown could be comfortable? "I'm fine. The doctor's just taking forever."

Although I hadn't had another dizzy spell since the disaster a few weeks ago, Owen was still paranoid. He'd been around more, which had been nice, since taking my dad's advice and doing more at the firehouse and taking fewer EMT shifts.

Owen's phone buzzed, and he pulled it from his pocket. "It's Mom again." He chuckled. "She's dying to know if it's a boy or a girl."

It had been fun hanging out with Owen's family last weekend, and the extra hands were a huge help with the move. Luckily, the complex had agreed to extend my lease and let Owen out of his early.

Although we had almost everything settled, we still had some organizing to do. And in about five weeks, I'd go to part-time hours, and I'd have more time to devote to it.

Owen sighed. "Now your dad is texting me too. He wants an update." He shook his head. "Is this a glimpse into how it's going to be when you go into labor?"

"Probab—" my words were cut short as I homed in on the

black speck moving along the edge of the exam table. "Ew," I squealed, scrambling off the table and into Owen's lap. I buried my face in his neck as he shifted, but I didn't dare look.

"Got it," he said as calmly as usual. Like this was a common occurrence. In all fairness, it kind of was.

I lifted my head. "I'm sorry. I really need to try not to freak out so much. I know it's silly."

"I'll never complain when spiders send Little Miss Muffet right into my arms."

I smiled and pressed my lips against his, then climbed back up on the table just as the doctor stepped into the room.

Once we had me situated with the goo and the wand was skating over my belly, our baby appeared on the screen.

"Whoa, look at our little guy." Owen leaned forward, his gaze intent on the screen. "You can really make out some of his features now.

"Did you want to know what you're having?" The look on my doctor's face as he asked made me wonder if my dad was right.

"Yes," we said in unison.

"It's a girl."

I laughed. "Of course it's a girl." We'd *just* painted the nursery navy blue. "Because nothing about this has gone to plan."

Owen smiled. "You know, someone once said the best things happen when plans go to shit."

Epilogue

Pregnancy Week One:

At least the second time it happens, you're actually trying for baby number two.

CeCe

I SMILED as Grace spun in circles, her long blond hair flowing around her.

"Daddy, Daddy. Bubbles." She ran up to me, a wand in her hand, and twirled again, releasing a chain of bubbles into the air, then she was off again.

"I can't believe she's two already." Danny shook his head.

My two best friends had made the trip down for my daughter's birthday, and that made the occasion even more perfect. Ever since Pete had gotten married, all three of our girls had become fast friends, so it made the times we could meet up even better.

"I still can't believe you fu—" Pete sputtered as his wife elbowed him in the side. "Right." He shook his head. "Language."

I chuckled.

"Can't believe you both have little humans now." He nodded at the kids as Grace continued to twirl while Danny's little one toddled around her.

Some days, I couldn't believe it either. But neither I nor Danny would have it any other way.

"Well, those things are a hit." Brian laughed as he stepped off the deck and into the backyard, where the small group was gathered.

"Yeah." Cece smiled. "Grace loves her bubbles. That's for sure."

I wrapped my arm around my wife, tucking her into my side.

"And the house is really coming together," Brian said. "The new furniture looks good."

Things were definitely falling into place. Brian had announced his plan to retire in the next five years, and he was grooming me to move into his position. When I was forced to move here, I'd given up on that dream. But now it looked like I'd skate in just under forty. We'd purchased the house shortly after Cece started her new job at the pediatric group. The office hours were the selling point for her.

"Don't mention the word furniture." Kelly laughed as she and Jack stepped up next to them. "I don't think I'm ever going to live that one down."

"You two ready for one of those yet?" I nodded toward the kids running around the yard.

Kelly smiled. "Jack wanted to be married for at least a year first, but I figure it will happen when it happens."

The group fell into easy conversation as I took it all in. Today had turned out to be pretty damn perfect. Even if my parents and sisters had headed back to Richmond an hour ago and my best friends were leaving tomorrow.

I had no complaints. I hugged Cece closer and pressed my lips to the top of her head.

My girls were my entire world.

PETER PUMPKINED OUT - SNEAK PEEK

1

Pete

"What do you mean 'strike'?"

On the other side of my desk, the president of operations raised his gray eyebrows and pursed his lips, reminding me of Uncle Gio. Alan Beria was one of just a handful of originals left from when Gio started All Out Brewing.

"Strike, as in no one will be delivering our beer." Alan folded his arms across his chest, tucking the folder stamped with the All Out logo surrounded by hops flowers under his right elbow. He was still an asset to the brewery, but damn, this old man was a pain in my ass. Although Gio had mentored me for years, I wasn't my uncle, so things had changed when I'd taken the helm. Alan glared at the phone in my hand, his dark eyes full of annoyance.

Oh hell, Owen was still on the line. I didn't have time to deal with my best friend's woman drama right now. He'd made his bed, and now he'd have to lie in it.

"Later, dick." I slammed the phone down without waiting for his response. Owen wouldn't care. He and Danny, my college roommates, were used to it. My best friends never expected nice. Unlike when I was forced to play the politically correct CEO of All Out, with friends, I was just me.

"Sorry, no matter what I say, Mr. Beria just barges in." Alice, my first line of defense when uninvited guests showed up, wrung her hands from the doorway. Behind thick glasses, her eyes flicked between us.

In my office, the rule was *no appointment, no meeting*. As much as I wished it did, that didn't apply to Alan, though. Uncle Gio's best friend was still entitled to some perks, even two years after Gio's death.

"It's fine." I waved her off.

The older woman nodded and closed the thick double door behind her, leaving us alone in my office.

A lot had changed in the twenty-five years that All Out Brewing had existed, but not much had been altered in this office since Gio moved the company's headquarters from the brewing warehouses in Long Island to midtown. For years, I'd watched and learned from my uncle, right here in this office. I'd sat where Alan sat now as my uncle explained the ins and outs of the industry. Studying the books on the shelves that lined one wall, surveying the city skyline through the massive windows behind the desk. It felt like home, so even though the space was a little outdated, I didn't want to change it, even now that I'd taken over the company.

The leather of the chair creaked as I stood. I propped one hip on the desk and scanned the skyline. It didn't matter what time of day it was; the streets were always hopping. People were constantly hurrying in and out of stores, restaurants, and bars. Bars that would be unable to serve our line of the best local craft brews if we didn't stop this strike from happening. What had once been a small startup was now one of the East Coast's largest brands, pumping out anywhere from fifteen to twenty unique beers each season.

"So the drivers are really doing this?" I spun back to Alan. "Can we replace them all?" There were a million people in this city. How hard could it be to find some schmuck to deliver beer?

Alan let out a long sigh and dropped his shoulders. "I warned you this was a possibility. We've been in contract negotiations for a month."

Exactly. The drivers were being unreasonable—more pay, less work; it was what everyone wanted these days. But a company didn't grow by wasting money.

Alan tossed the folder onto my desk. The manila lid flapped as it bounced on the dark wood. "They've been working without a contract, and you've been refusing to budge on their demands. This was inevitable." Rubbing his hand over his neatly trimmed salt and pepper beard, he glared down at the envelope. "That's twenty-five temporary replacements. Pick eighteen for tomorrow, otherwise we'll need to cancel orders."

"Like hell we'll cancel anything." I opened the folder and flipped through a couple of candidates, then tossed the stack back on the desk. "Have Alice call them. The first eighteen that confirm get the job. How hard is it to drop off beer?"

Alan crossed his arms over his slight beer gut. "Maybe avoid leading with that tomorrow."

Cocking a brow, I stood to my full six-foot height and looked down at him.

"They're willing to sit down at nine a.m.," he said. "Consider giving a little so we can get these guys back on the clock. Our biggest issue shouldn't be who the hell is going to deliver our product."

"Exactly." I let out a snort.

Thirty minutes into the meeting, things were going poorly. I was annoyed, but I wasn't stupid. I recognized the horrible turn this meeting was taking. Alan sat at the opposite end of the large conference table, glaring at me. Between our people and the drivers' representatives, there were twelve of us crammed into the windowless room, and it was starting to get hot.

Craig loosened his tie and cleared his throat. Our in-house counsel was doing a shit job mediating this circus. If he used the word *compromise* one more time, I would fire him, regardless of Alan's ranting about it. Alan was being a pussy about these negotiations. We had to hold our ground rather than let these buffoons walk all over us. There was no way in hell I was going to let them drive my uncle's company into the ground.

"We're not saying we're unwilling to acquiesce to any of your demands." Alan sent me a pointed look, but that was exactly what I was saying.

He and I needed to get on the same page. I refused to agree to fewer deliveries daily. If I did, we'd have to hire more full-time drivers and purchase more trucks and delivery equipment. That was out of the question. Along with their easier workdays, they were demanding higher pay and additional vacation time. Regardless of how sympathetic Alan was to these guys, we were already spending too much money on the easiest part of the operation. We would not bleed out over the details of delivering our products.

"We're not asking you to reinvent the wheel here," I said, scooting forward in my seat. "We're just asking you to run your routes on time and do it with A+ customer service." I internally rolled my eyes, hating the term my uncle had coined. A rating scale for successful deliveries was unnecessary. Get there on time, drop off the right beer, stack it nicely, and get out without leaving a mess. Rocket science it was not.

"Fifteen drops by the eleven-a.m. hard stop is virtually impossible. Not with the way the routes are laid out." The union rep tossed his hands up in the air.

Stupid-ass rule. "No restaurant is so busy that it can't accept deliveries between eleven and one." The drop-off guidelines made no sense.

"Whoa, whoa, let's not get upset here." Craig was a jack wad. We were here today because we were all upset. "It's not the fault of the drivers' union or All Out. That's a restaurant industry rule."

No shit, asshole. Craig really wasn't worth the money I was paying him.

"If we can take it down to twelve deliveries before lunch, plus make some headway on the vacation time and pay scale, I'd think we'd have 90 percent compliance." The union rep leaned forward and zeroed in on me.

"I refuse to believe fifteen isn't possible," I said, pulling my shoulders back.

Alan was glaring again. It was like tiny needles being shot across the room. He was sure his experience made him better equipped to make the decision about the drivers' contract. Arrogance was hard to work with.

Vince, one of All Out's best drivers, cleared his throat. "If anyone could do it, you could, right?" He smirked, resting his thick forearms on the table as he leaned into the conversation.

"I don't have time to do my job and yours."

I didn't even have time for this. I should have been in my office going over the new formulas, approving the budgets for next year, testing the upcoming season's brew, and studying forecasts.

"Not every day," he said, cocking a thick, unkept brow, "but you could do it once, right?" The glint in Vince's brown eyes was all challenge. "If you were to run my route tomorrow..."

"I could do it one handed." On a normal day, I ran circles around our entire staff. My day started at five a.m. and ended around nine p.m., and that was if I didn't have a business dinner to work into my schedule. One delivery shift would be nothing.

Alan pushed his chair back and stood. "Hold up."

With a huff, I waved him off.

Vince leaned to one side and whispered to the union rep. The guy nodded and sat a little straighter.

"Okay, you run the route tomorrow. The full route. If you have no complaints, then we'll meet back here on Friday and sign the contract you've presented."

It couldn't be that easy, could it? Regardless, I wouldn't argue. "Sounds like a deal."

CHAPTER 1

As the room cleared, Alan pulled me aside. "This is a horrible idea. Have you ever driven a truck? Tapped a keg?"

"I went to college, you know." I'd tapped more kegs in my first year of college than the drivers did in a week.

Alan sighed. "Setting up a kegerator or a rent-a-tap isn't anything like what our guys do. Most of our customers are massive sports bars with multi-page purchase orders."

Rolling my eyes, I brushed past him. I had shit to get done if I was going to spend the following morning making deliveries.

"Do you even know how to read a purchase order?" It was time Alan moved on from his old-school worrywart ways. My uncle may have been fine with it, but All Out was moving forward, and I didn't work that way.

"Jesus, I work with budgets. How hard could it be?"

"Famous last words."

***

Want more of Pete & Cara ?
Grab Peter Pumpkined Out now!

ALSO BY GRACIE YORK

AJ RANNEY & JENNI BARA

Gracie York Books:

Goldilocks and the Grumpy Bear

Tumbling Head Over Heels

Along Came The Girl

Peter Pumpkined Out

Jenni Bara Books:

More Than The Game

More Than Fine

More Than A Hero

More Than A Story

More Than Myself

Mother Maker (coming 2024)

AJ Ranney Books:

Always Yours

Wishing to be Yours

Impossibly Yours

Imperfectly Yours (coming 2024)

Thank You

Dear Reader (Jenni here),

When I dropped a pen name into *More than a Hero* for my character Morgan, AJ knew we needed to bring Gracie York's stories to life. Convincing me to do it with her was the easy part because I'm always willing to change directions and focus on something new. Anyone else have attention spam problems, or is it just me?

Gracie's debut novel came from the fact that we wanted to write our favorite tropes first. I thought we meant grumpy/sunshine, all the while, AJ was thinking we were doing snowed in. Then in the middle of the night, I came up with the crazy idea that we could make it Goldilocks, and I texted this to AJ. She, of course, thought I meant going a whole new way. But once I explained (in the morning at a reasonable hour), she loved the idea. And Goldilocks and the Grumpy Bear was born. Which then paved the way to our theme of funny smutty versions of popular nursery rhymes.

After releasing Tumbling Head over Heels this winter, we enjoyed Jack and Kelly so much we had to rejoin their world and find a match for Kelly's bestie. Hopefully you love Owen as much as we did. And to add to the fun Owen's best friend just gets to be one of my Evan brothers.

So now that Goldilocks got snowed in with the Grumpy Bear, and Jack brought Jill up the hill with him before

Tumbling Head Over Heels together, and a spider sent Little Miss Muffet straight into Owen's arms what are we doing next? This fall, we'll pumpkin out the year with Peter, Peter, Pumpkin Eater. And then we are going to find a perfect match for the little lady who lives with too many kids in a shoe. We would love to have you join us for the entire trip.

Happy reading.

Acknowledgments

Thank you to our wonderful readers, whose love for our characters sometimes even outweighs our own. Your love for the Metros men, the Evans family, and all the characters from Half Moon Lake is amazing. To our street and ARC teams, a big thank you for all your sharing, your reviews, your support, your shout-outs. You are all the best!

Thank you to our families for all your support and love. We couldn't do this without you! A special thank you too Ashley and Will for dealing with our constant phone calls to plot or tweak the things that aren't working. We know we annoy you both.

Beth, thank you for being so flexible and understanding with this book and everything. We are so glad we found you, and we will never stop singing your praises from the rooftop. You are amazing with your edits and proofreads and checking everything twice! You are thoughtful and detailed and amazing at keeping an author's voice. More than that, you are a friend who Jenni is so grateful to have in her life. Thank you for being the wonderful person you are.

Katie, thank you for all your endless help and support. You've been with Jenni since the start and added AJ along the way. We both love all your edits, comments, and suggestions. Without you, our stories would never be what they are.

Haley, thank you so much for all your help. Words can't

express how grateful we are for what you do. Jenni's constant "wait, I have a new plan/idea" that makes you pivot never fazes you, and AJ's schedules and need for a plan you make work too. We couldn't be more different and yet equally frustrating, and you take it all in stride.

Erica, thank you for all you do. You are the blurb master and the graphics queen. We never stop learning from you. Jenni can't express how thankful she is for all you do to teach and support her.

Daphne and Britt, thank you for being friends and teachers. The amount of knowledge and insight you have given is something that we are eternally grateful for. And your friendship is something we don't want to do without. Even the funny parts like Britt reading Jenni's thoughts. You two are the best. Everyone should check out the Havenport Series by Daphne Elliot and the Bristol Bay series by Brittanee Nicole because these two women have too much talent to not be known to every reader.

Annie, thank you for your cover help. You are never fazed by all the SOS help or the fact that half a world away, you are teaching wraps. And on top of that, you never hesitate to make time for a beta read. You rock! And everyone should check out The Temptation Series by Annie Charms.

And thank you, Amy Jo, for not only beta reading, but for all the beautiful book minis, bookmarks, and other swag you've made for us.

To all our author friends and beta readers, thank you for being supportive and inspiring writers. Kristin Lee, Alexandra Hale, Swati MH, Amanda Zook, Bonnie Poirier, JL Reed, Garry Michaels, Kat Long, Jane Poller, Lizzie Stanley, Blye Donovan, Raleigh Damson, Bethany Monaco Smith, Elyse Kelly, and so many, many more.

Jeff, thank you for being the final nit-picky check to make

sure everything is perfect. Becoming a romance reader wasn't on your to-do list, but Jenni's grateful you did it anyway!

To all our friends and family, a big thank you because we love you, and your support is something we are eternally thankful to have.

About the Authors

AJ fell in love with Morgan's pen name, Gracie York, from *More than a Hero* and talked Jenni into bringing her books to life. Gracie York was born as a real-life author, and the two began co-writing. AJ is the plotter, organizer, and planner, so she writes all the bones of the story, then sends it back to Jenni. Then, when AJ is busy with her two kids, husband, and her house full of animals, Jenni goes through to add, edit, and tweak it. Which sometimes includes line editing her own sentences more than a few times to make it all just right. Then while AJ works on more bones, Jenni goes back to her four kids and day job as a paralegal in family law, writing real life unhappily ever afters all day. AJ and Jenni have not only become co-authors but great friends, and they can't wait to bring more of Gracie York's stories to life.

Printed in Great Britain
by Amazon